ADAM'S

13513

Also by Alison Rush
THE LAST OF DANU'S CHILDREN

ADAM'S PARADISE

Alison Rush

MACMILLAN CHILDREN'S BOOKS

First published 1988 by
MACMILLAN CHILDREN'S BOOKS
A division of Macmillan Publishers Limited
London and Basingstoke
Associated companies throughout the world

Paperback edition published 1989

ISBN 0-333-46268-8

A CIP catalogue record for this book is available from the British Library

Typeset by Matrix, London WC2

Printed in Hong Kong

Chapter 1

Twilight caught Ruth unawares that night. As she reached Starr Hills the sun was a misty red disc over the sea, and there was rain in the air. It was a poor summer that year. Black rainclouds were riding up from the south, killing the light and making the day seem almost over. Wind muttered in the marram grass; the tide was out, and the estuary was like a hollow hand spread to receive the night.

She surveyed Starr Hills. It was the first time she'd come here in seven years, and this deserted expanse of dunes on the northern point of the estuary seemed bigger than she remembered, and more desolate. The seaward dunes were shifting and unstable, spiked thinly with the marram that hereabouts was called starr grass, giving the place its name. Inland, the hills were fixed now under their carpet of coarse heath grass, gorse and small flowers. As the sun set, pools of darkness were growing in the innumerable dips and hollows.

Nothing had changed. The locals still used the place as a tip, and piles of old tyres and other junk lay about. No one came here for pleasure. It was haunted, of course, by the ghost of a witch's daughter; the sea had risen up while

1

she walked along the shore here, and swept her away because of her wickedness. But Ruth had come to find her brother, not look for ghosts.

She found the place without difficulty. A dumped car lay in one of the wet slacks – wheel-less, both wings dented and the windscreen gone. Ruth opened the creaking rear door and climbed in. Her brother Adam's old green waterproof lay on the seat.

Ruth sat hunched, knees drawn up under her chin, and waited.

The rain came in flurries, dulling the dusk to a bleak monochrome. What a place to be . . . and yet that evening she'd suddenly felt certain it was where she'd find Adam. It was queer, how well she still knew him. For seven years they'd lived apart – Adam in Wickrithe with Gran, herself in Coniston with Aunt Sarah and Uncle Nick – but now that she was back in Wickrithe, helping Gran with her bed-and-breakfast business for the summer, it was as if there'd been no break. It was frightening, how easy it was to slip back into the past.

She didn't like Wickrithe. The place was too full of memories; like the day she'd discovered most kids had mothers, not just a gran. And the day, not long afterwards, when she'd first heard someone call her father crazy. At school she and Adam had been the different ones, the Demdykes – the ones with a dead mother and a crazy father. It had been almost a relief when, just after her eighth birthday, her father had disappeared.

"He's gone, love," Gran had said shortly, when asked. "None knows where. 'Twas allus sure he would, sometime . . ."

She remembered how Adam, seven years old and already stronger-willed than anyone could cope with, had furiously affirmed that Jake would come back. When Aunt Sarah arrived, proposing to take them both to live with her in Coniston, he had utterly refused to go.

Ruth had gone, numbly obeying the grown-ups. And she still remembered how, as the car began to climb into the lakeland hills, she had seen her first mountain – a sharp blue crag that, outlined against the sky, had made her sit up and stare. It had come to her, then, that there were places different from Wickrithe. By the time they reached Coniston and she saw grey stone cottages beside a lake reflecting more of those unbelievable mountains, she knew she was being offered a new world. No one in Coniston talked about crazy Demdykes; and her cousins, Robin and Jenny, seemed to like her and want to be friends. Gradually, miraculously, she had found herself free of her past.

In time, the idea of fetching Adam to join her had lapsed. "I don't like leaving him with Ma," Aunt Sarah said occasionally, worried. "She's enough to do, with her bed-and-breakfasts. And it's not as if he's an easy lad."

But Adam always refused to move. "Let him be," Uncle Nick said at last. "He knows what he wants, and that's more than most folk do."

So Adam had been let be. Wickrithe was only two hours away by car, and every so often they drove down to spend an afternoon with Gran; but usually Adam was nowhere to be seen. Ruth played games with Robin and Jenny in Gran's garden, and if Adam did appear,

3

scowling and unkempt, somehow he never joined in. He seemed to inhabit his own world, set apart from them; and Ruth hardly remembered it had once been her world too.

But now, looking out at the gusty darkening waste, she did remember. In the old days she and Adam had often come to Starr Hills; it was lonely, with no one to shout "Crazy Demdykes" after them, and they'd played intense, obsessive games of treasure-hunting amongst the junk. But it's just a foul old tip, Ruth thought; why do we still have to come here?

Adam had disappeared two days ago. It happened a lot, Ruth knew; Gran said tartly that he'd be back when he was hungry enough. But Ruth was getting scared about him. She'd known he was growing up peculiar – he did badly at school, and had no friends – but she'd begun to see, from living in the same house as him again, how different he was from other kids. There were days when you just couldn't talk to him, when he stared at you as if what you said made no sense, and then gave you answers you couldn't understand. Often he seemed desperate, violent, as if thrashing around inside himself for certainties that weren't there. Frequently Ruth wondered why he hadn't ended up in borstal or some other institution. But in the legal sense she supposed he did nothing worse than truant from school.

Except that now he'd stolen the cup Crazy Jake, their father, had given her. And that was a mean thing to do; it was just a shabby little metal cup, and she couldn't remember when or why Jake had put it into her hands. She wasn't even sure how it had found its way into the suitcase she packed for Wickrithe. But somehow it stuck to her, a battered meaningless fragment of those far-off days, something that until now she'd never quite managed to lose.

She waited, shutting her eyes and shivering as the light waned. Presently she heard footsteps slipping on the wet grass, and then one of the doors groaned open. She looked up.

"Have you got any food?" said Adam hoarsely, hunching up sideways in the driver's seat.

He looked gaunt and exhausted, but fierce-eyed still. His dark hair was full of tangles. How like him, Ruth thought, to come and hole up in a dumped car on Starr Hills. Looking at him now, she guessed this was what he always did when he disappeared.

"I don't care if you starve," she said tightly, slipping back into the rough gibing of their childhood. "Give me back Crazy Jake's cup. And don't dare say you didn't take it!"

Adam gave her an uncomprehending stare. "I am starving. I hadn't time to bring any food. And it's cold as death here at night. As soon as I get to sleep, I dream I'm at the bottom of the sea." He drew his knees up to his chest and coughed. "Haven't you got *anything* to eat?"

Ruth sighed irritably and rummaged in her pocket for a chocolate bar. Gran kept her supplied with them, on the grounds that she was too thin. "That's all I've got. I want the cup, Adam!"

"You can't have it," said Adam, seizing the chocolate. "Crazy Jake's back. And he wants it."

Ruth was silent from pure shock. Crazy Jake, here

5

again? Seven years ago he'd gone away, leaving her nothing but the cup to remember him by; it was so long ago that Crazy Jake, with his wide strange eyes and his queer stories, seemed more like a creature from a dream than a flesh-and-blood father. "If he ain't dead, he's in jail," Ruth had once overheard Gran saying sourly to Aunt Sarah. "He'll not be back. He's gone, my Jake. I know it in me bones."

"He can't be!" she said. "He's – gone . . . "

Adam gave her a scornful look, licking the last crumbs of chocolate from the paper. "They all say that. Because they don't want him back. He scares them. He's here all right – I met him on the shore two nights ago. He told me to come back, and bring the cup."

Ruth felt herself shivering. She wasn't a Wickrithe girl any more; she belonged to Coniston, and Uncle Nick was more her father than Jake had ever been. But . . . "What's he like?" she asked.

"Madder than ever. Why don't you go back to Gran's? You don't want to meet him."

Ruth hugged her arms tightly, remembering she was a year older than Adam. And if Crazy Jake was back – her own father . . . But it was no good. "Adam, let's both go back," she said pleadingly. "There's no point doing what he says if he's still mad."

"Go back to that bloody town? Not me! If crazy Jake can leave it, so can I, and I'd rather be mad like him than sane like that lot in Wickrithe!"

That convinced Ruth Jake really was back. Otherwise, Adam would never have talked about leaving Wickrithe.

She said, low, "Where's he been, Adam?"

6

"You wouldn't believe it if I told you," Adam said, and gave a sudden mirthless laugh. "I don't know if I believe it myself yet. If he comes back tonight I'm going to end up madder than him. Come on, let's go and look for him."

He scrambled out of the car and led the way to the new dunes overlooking the sea. Ruth followed. The sun was down and the night wind boomed in the great hollow shell of the estuary. Climbing the highest dune behind Adam, Ruth looked in vain for stars; black clouds covered the entire sky.

"Out there's where I met him," said Adam, nodding towards the shore.

Ruth stared. The tide had turned; she could see the white caps approaching. Otherwise there was nothing. "Where did he come from?" she asked.

Adam gave his harsh crack of laughter again. "Wait and see. He's got to come tonight. If he thinks I can stand another night in that car, he's even madder than I thought."

Ruth hunched herself against the wind. She was beginning to feel queer and sick; it was as if the sandhills were moving, swinging under her feet, and the sky going noiselessly round. Her head hurt. "Adam," she said weakly, "let's go home ..."

She saw his profile, dark and eager beside her. "Not likely," he said, and circling ripples puckered the surface of the sky. "He's *coming*!" Adam shouted, and the dunes bucked like horses.

Ruth found herself on her knees, sand rasping between her fingers. The sky whipped like a rag on a clothes-line, and the sea roared white up the shore. She saw Adam stumble.

Something with a dull gleam flew from his hand, tumbling down the slope of the dune. It spun as it went, and at once the spinning of earth and sky seemed to centre on it, as if on a vortex. Ruth hurled herself after it, or perhaps was hurled – she didn't know. But she knew that the thing which fell, the thing with the faint pewterish gleam, was Crazy Jake's cup.

She clasped it, landing at the foot of the dune with her face in the wet grass. Her hands knew it, old worn cool metal with rubbed-away beading round the rim. Presently she felt the sick spinning of the hills sink away into a taut stillness. She slid the cup into a pocket of her waterproof and raised her head.

Next moment she was caught in a strong arm, a hand coming over her mouth. For one wild moment she thought it was Adam fighting her for the cup; but it was a more powerful arm that pinned her. She saw the man's eyes, staring round the side of the dune towards the sea.

She kicked, struggled; but he seemed almost not to notice, staring across the darkening shore. Ruth managed a strangled sound through his hand, praying Adam would hear.

The man looked down at her at once, and she saw his face. She froze, unable to believe . . . He was a big man of about forty, with dark hair flopping over his forehead; his eyes were dark too, strangely wide and clear like a child's; and his face was as familiar to her as Adam's. She had never realized before that Adam had grown to look so like his father.

He whispered, "Oh hush, hush, will you? If they find me, it means my death!"

Ruth couldn't have spoken, even if he had moved his hand. Was it true? Could it really be her father, gripping her in his arms after seven years? But all she could feel was a cold overpowering daze; seven years was too long; she didn't know what to do.

He glanced across the shore again, and even in the dark she could see lines deepen round his mouth. "Will you not make a sound?" he whispered pleadingly. "To let me live through the night, lassie, will you stay quiet?"

It was Jake; that was the very lilt of his craziness. Ruth nodded dumbly. He took his hand from her mouth, and she stared up into his queer, childlike eyes; but the more she looked, the less childish those eyes seemed, the sadder and more desperate. Indeed, there was a moment when they seemed the oldest eyes in the world.

His brows drew together, uneasy at her scrutiny. Then he whispered, awkwardly, "I came to meet my son. And to fetch a cup that my daughter keeps safe for me . . . "

Ruth swallowed. Didn't he know her? He was so clearly mad, she wasn't sure; but the mere thought hurt unbelievably, her eyes going hot with tears. He'd known Adam, hadn't he? Then why not her too? "Madder than ever," she recalled Adam saying, and she turned her head away roughly, bitter at having such a madman for a father. Remembering the cup in her pocket, she pressed her hand over the flap to hide it.

She could feel him hesitating, shoulders hunching with the sense of something wrong. Then all at once he

9

stiffened, staring again towards the shore. Ruth looked, feeling her heart thump.

The sky was dark, except for a patch of pearl in the west. The wind had strengthened, and there was more rain too, blowing in swirls. Wherever she looked, movements caught at the edge of her vision.

"They don't see so well," Jake whispered, "but they can hear the mere beat of a man's heart!"

They? Jake seemed in the grip of a madness deeper than any Ruth remembered; all she wanted now, overwhelmingly, was to get away from him. *I'm Ruth, your daughter*, she thought; *I've got the cup you wanted, and Adam's here too somewhere* . . . But she couldn't say it. Suppose he was too mad to understand her? The hurt would be even worse then.

Another movement flickered, and halfway up a dune something seemed to vanish – she saw, clearly, the sand slide and some bent starr grass spring back. Her heart seemed to go climbing up inside her chest, but it wasn't till Jake's hand clamped over her mouth again that she realized she'd been about to scream.

"Oh, hush!" There was a queer pity in his voice. "Did you see them, poor lass?"

Ruth forced back the scream; it felt horrible, like trying not to be sick. "No. Not *see*. But there was something there – wasn't there?"

"Aye. There was, lass." Jake gazed across the dim dunes again, still gripping her in his arm: and it felt now as if he held her just for comfort – his own, perhaps, as much as hers. The rain came on harder, and what with that and the darkness, Ruth could scarcely see anything. But then she seemed to hear, from a huge distance, a thin desolate

10

calling like gulls high up in the sky.

They were too faint to see properly, and gone as soon as seen. Only long cloaks blowing, up on top of the young dunes, a gaze of strange cold eyes, a flash of spear-points – then the rain drove across, and Ruth could see only night.

Jake made a whispering noise, half a sigh and half a groan. "Lords of light! If only I had understanding, to send them back to their waters!"

Ruth was beginning to feel it was all just a dream; part of her mind felt detached, quite separate from her body. "Can't we run?" she whispered. "It's not far back to the town!"

"Too far for me, lass," Jake murmured. "I've come too far from the ways of men to be able to go back now . . . but we must get away from that sea!" He rose swiftly, holding out his hand. "Come, now. They've the deep sea still in their eyes, they'll not glimpse us yet."

Ruth looked at him – the gentle, desperate face, the powerful shoulders under the old coat. There was a weird mixture of strength and helplessness in him. But now that it was possible to run away from him, she didn't want to. She took his hand and, with a sense of stepping from the present into the past, from the known into what had become utterly strange, scrambled up and ran after him into the night.

A tallish hummock loomed, and he pulled her down into the wet grass behind it. She guessed they'd come about twenty yards inland; she could still hear the sigh and fall of the incoming tide. Where was Adam? She felt the presences of whatever she'd seen, like a cold breath on her spine.

She whispered, "What are they?"

11

Jake looked at her helplessly. "I'm afraid to tell you. Lass, I don't know how to."

Ruth made herself say it. "Are they – real?" As she spoke she felt as if she were stepping into Jake's craziness, becoming part of it. She heard again that faint cold calling, like gulls far up in the sky – half a sound, half a shiver over the skin. She hadn't known it was possible to feel so afraid.

"They're real, but not like us," Jake whispered, then turned his head away like a shamefaced child. "Perhaps it's only I who call them! They come from the sea at night, when the tide flows – or in a sea mist."

He's mad, he's mad, Ruth thought; but she dared not leave him. Every sound of the wind and rain seemed now like footsteps or the faint rattle of spears. She squeezed her eyes tight shut, then opened them again, knowing what she'd see.

He was climbing down one of the young dunes, slowly, feeling with the butt of his spear like a blind man – a thing as substanceless as a swirl of rain. His helmet seemed to burn with a faint silver flame, the folds of his cloak drifted round him like water, and his eyes were cold and lost like someone in a dream. Even as Ruth tried to tell herself it was impossible, she saw more – a crowd, a host of them, spears glinting in the rain.

"That I should fail Undry so!" Jake whispered, with a break in his voice. Ruth had no idea what he meant, but she felt pierced; she remembered the cup in her pocket and was conscious of a need to fight through her fear, grip the cup, hand it to her father. But she couldn't; she was paralysed.

Jake's hands gripped her shoulders. "I must go," he whispered. "I must draw these shadows back into the sea, where they can hurt less. Find my son; find Adam. Tell him Undry must be returned — "

"Oh no," Ruth whispered. "Don't go!"

"There has been enough of me in your life, child!" In that instant it came to Ruth that he *did* know her; but before she could be sure his hands left her shoulders and he went leaping round the side of the hummock, his long coat flapping, straight towards the spearmen. His voice shouted out, deep, full-throated, *"Go out of this world! Go back under the sea!"*

All the air shrilled, and it was as if a great wave broke over her. She saw them then, with shattering clarity; they crowded the dunes in a cold eddying radiance, each spear-point a spark of light, grimly staring as if from a trance. One of them cried out, in a fierce voice like a seagull's, and all the spears lifted. Then another voice cut through the shrilling, raw and shaken – *"Father!"* And she saw Adam start up from the starr grass.

Jake checked only for an instant. Then he broke through the host like a great dark flapping bird, and Adam flung himself after him. The voices rose to a piercing shriek, and the crowd of silver helmets went flooding in pursuit, chasing both of them down the dunes to the sea. Ruth saw thrown spears hang in the air as if floating in water, and she thrust herself down into the grass, her face in her hands so as not to see any more.

She didn't know how time passed, or how long it took the wild shrill crying to fade back into the sky; but at last there was just the sound of the rain and the wind. She sat up. The clouds had begun to roll back, and the darkness went with them, revealing a sky pink with sunset. Presently the rain stopped, and the evening was calm and clear.

She looked at her watch. It was only a quarter to nine; not night-time at all. Stiffly, feeling like an old woman, she got to her feet and trudged between the hummocks till she reached the top of one of the new dunes on the shoreline. Before her the sea rippled placidly in, dark blue with rosy glints reflecting the sunset. Of the silver-helmed spearmen, of Jake and Adam, there was no sign.

She stood there. For a long time it felt as if that was all she could do. She couldn't *think*; her mind had stopped doing that sort of thing; she could only wait till her arms and legs felt like moving again. Presently, without taking any conscious decision about it, she climbed down the dune and began to search Starr Hills for Jake and Adam.

Chapter 2

Ruth got into bed and sat there, knees drawn up under the covers. Holding Jake's cup in her hands, she inspected it minutely.

She'd never really looked at it before; it was too old and familiar. Just a small bowl, about the size of a teacup; made of a dull pewterish metal, leaf-thin with age; decorated with some worn beading round the rim, and on the sides a formal pattern of entwining lines. Without knowing why, Ruth had always felt there was something unfinished about it. The pattern seemed less than it should be – incomplete, provisional.

It was, she realized, a peculiar thing to own. She'd never seen anything like it in other people's houses, or in shops - not even antique shops. It's more like something from a museum, she thought. A remote, glass-encased thing you couldn't touch . . . Perhaps it actually was very old – an old forgotten secretive thing, so old even its purpose had been forgotten. Where had Jake got it from? Why did he now want it back? Almost completely rubbed away in places, the lines twined round the bowl like a knot no one could untie.

It was eleven o'clock. She'd found no trace of Jake or

Adam on Starr Hills; and she'd returned to Gran's into the usual evening bustle of getting ready for next morning's breakfasts. That solved, temporarily, the problem of what to tell Gran; there was no chance to say anything. But now she knew she had to think and decide what to do.

She put Jake's cup away in her bedside locker. Overwhelmingly, she didn't want to believe any of it had happened; her instinct was to block it out of her mind, to pretend she'd never seen Adam and Jake, much less a host of silver-helmed spearmen ... But Adam was her own brother, Jake her own father; she had to do something to find them. What, she didn't know. *I never do know*, she thought. *I'm useless in a crisis.*

She'd realized recently that she didn't like herself much. She was dull. Stodgy. Stick-in-the-muddish. Robin and Jenny were the ones who had adventures, fell-walking or sailing on the lake, always coming home with hair-raising stories; but nothing ever happened to Ruth. She enjoyed cooking, and sewing, and listening to other people's adventures. People liked her because she was steady, sensible, a good listener. She was dull.

Which made her the last person to know how to handle this evening's adventure. *I can't* tell anyone, she thought; *people wouldn't believe me, they'd just pat my hand and give me tranquillizers. Even Gran'd think I was off my head.* In fact she *felt* off her head, her mind a sickening unaccustomed whirl. Well, she decided at last, *if Adam doesn't turn up tomorrow I'll go and look for him and Jake again on Starr Hills. But if I can't find them, or anything else happens – I'll phone home. I'll think of*

16

some way to ask Aunt Sarah or Uncle Nick what to do, without telling them the crazy part. They'll help.

It was said in Wickrithe that all Demdykes were crazy, but Aunt Sarah disproved that. She wasn't perfect; she had a temper, and children who got in her way on bad days were liable to get clouted; but she was as normal as daylight and, for all her temper, the nicest person Ruth knew. Uncle Nick came a close second, Robin and Jenny joint thirds; thinking of them all, Ruth ached with home-sickness. It seemed cold, back in that old house in Wickrithe where the first years of her life had been spent.

Her bedroom was in the basement. Some years ago, Gran had converted the basement into a private flat, to leave the rest of the house for the guests. It had been a novelty at first, to sleep below ground level, footsteps passing on the pavement above her. But tonight it felt cold, claustrophobic, down there.

She heard Gran's shuffling step on the stairs. Then her door was opened, and Gran came in with a cup of tea for her.

"There you are, me love. Eh . . . " She sighed, sitting down stiffly on the chair by the wall. "Them stairs get no easier."

"Thanks," said Ruth, taking the tea. She wasn't fond of it as a rule, but tonight it tasted hot and reassuring. "Is your rheumatism playing you up, Gran?"

"Aye," said Gran, and rubbed her knee. "I don't know how I'd cope, wi'out you to help, lass. It's the rain bringing it on. Rain! I've not known owt like it this summer!"

"Typical holiday weather," said Ruth. She looked at

17

Gran, feeling once again that faint curious shock at how she'd aged. It seemed to have happened in a rush, just recently; Ruth still thought of her as the upright, vigorous Gran of her childhood. But she was smaller now, and her shoulders had become bent, her hair thin and wispy. It was because of her worsening rheumatism that she'd asked for Ruth to come and help her this summer.

"Aye, well, folks that come to Wickrithe for their holidays should be used to it," Gran said. "They was saying in the grocer's today, the river'll be flooding if it gets much worse. I tell 'em, that's all I need, to wake up and find me bed floating off up the stairs."

Ruth grinned at that. But at the same time, she felt a faint chill; if there really was a flood, a basement like this wasn't the best place to be. "It's never happened before, has it?" she asked.

"Not as I recall," said Gran. "There's stories. They say a whole village got swept away once – and a church, another time. You're supposed to be able to hear its bells ringing under the sea at New Year's Eve." Unexpectedly, the lines deepened on her face. "Your father allus said he heard it, every year."

Ruth tensed. Jake . . . Gran talked about him a lot and, Ruth guessed, thought about him even more. She saw the lines scoring Gran's face – the same harsh lines that came when the rheumatism was at its worst. Somehow, they brought out in Gran a likeness to Jake and Adam, less in the features than in the look of the eyes, wide and clear like a passionate girl's.

"It'll never end," Gran said, her voice coming sudden and hard. "It'll never end, the trouble he's brought me.

18

There's that brother of yours, off searching for him again. Ach, he'll never learn ... He'll not find my Jake, no more'n my Jake'll ever find that woman he's after ... "

Ruth stared. Woman? Jake? "What woman?" she said blankly.

Gran looked at her sharply. "Why, your mother, of course, girl," she said testily.

Ruth felt as if she could do nothing but stare. The moment seemed to go on for ever, impossibly long-drawn-out. It wasn't shock, exactly; the world just seemed to withdraw to a vast, echoing distance. "But she's dead," she eventually heard herself point out, flat and toneless as if she wasn't much interested. "She's dead, Gran."

Gran's eyes widened. "Oh, my lovey ... " The words sank into silence. She gazed at Ruth, and her face seemed to fill up with horror. Pushing herself to her feet, she came to the bed in a stiff, hasty stumble; her arms went round Ruth, holding her tight. "Oh, my lovey," the old voice repeated over and over again, whispery with dismay. "Oh, my lovey ... "

Ruth drew in a breath. Her mind felt frozen; she didn't know what to do. Absurdly, it seemed most important to soothe Gran, and she reached up to squeeze her arm. "It's all right, Gran. I didn't mean to make a fuss; I – just really did think she was dead."

Gran sat stiffly on the bed, her face creased and distraught. "Oh, my lovey. All these years?"

Ruth nodded.

"Did you never hear different from your Aunt Sarah?"

"Not that I can remember," said Ruth. It was hard to

speak; deep down, she wanted Gran to stop, just go away and forget her mother had ever been mentioned. That frozen feeling seemed to have reached her heart, turning it cold and heavy like a stone.

"I can see how it was," said Gran. "You were always strange about your mother, lovey, even as a little lass. If ever I mentioned her, you'd just close up on me – turn away, like, as if you didn't hear. As if you *couldn't* hear. Sarah said once it was the same wi' her."

Ruth bit her lip. She couldn't remember ever doing that, not deliberately. But it's the kind of thing I would do, she thought, despising herself. Robin and Jenny both told her she shut her eyes to things she didn't like.

"But you're hearing now," said Gran, looking at her shrewdly.

"Yes," said Ruth. Her throat tightened on the word, as if even now she couldn't quite admit it; and she wondered how many other times she'd made herself not hear. She shivered. The thought was somehow shaming.

Gran sighed. "We should've known there was something wrong, lovey, the way you'd go deaf on us. Fancy me just blurting out about her, never thinking. But happen it's for the best; you had to know some time. I've told the lad about your mother time and again. 'Twas the only story he'd have from me at his bedtime, before he was grown ... " Her voice turned tired, wandering slightly like a very old woman's. "I ne'er liked telling it that way, like a fairy tale; but he's allus been that strong-willed ... "

Story? Was there more to it, then, than just the plain fact that her mother was still alive? She didn't want to know; she had Aunt Sarah; she didn't need a mother.

But . . . against her will, she heard herself saying, "What story, Gran?"

"No," said Gran at once, voice strengthening. "Poor lass, it's been enough, me coming out wi' summat like that wi'out warning. You've no need o' more, this time o' night." She pushed herself clumsily to her feet. "You lie down and get yourself off to sleep, now. That'll do you more good nor owt else."

Ruth hesitated. No, she told herself; I don't want to know! By this time what can any of it possibly matter? She lay down silently, pulling the covers over herself to get warm.

"There now," said Gran. "There's nowt more to tell, lass. Your mother left us after the lad was born, and she's ne'er been seen since. If you thought she was dead, there's no difference. She'll not be back . . . Don't you start fretting after her, now. You're best where you are, wi' my Sarah."

Of course she was. That was sense. "I'm all right, Gran," Ruth said.

"That's the way," said Gran, and put her knotted hand strongly on to Ruth's, gripping. "I'm nobbut an old fool, lass. Will you sleep now?"

Ruth summoned up a smile. "Yes. Of course."

"That's my lass," said Gran. "Goodnight then, lovey."

"Goodnight, Gran."

Taking the empty teacup, Gran went out, switching the light off and closing the door. Ruth heard the old footsteps shuffling away.

She lay looking bleakly at the darkness. Her only

coherent thought was that she should never have come back to stay in Wickrithe. Of course she'd had to; Gran needed her; Adam was no use, and Ruth, steady and sensible, was the obvious grandchild to come and help over the summer season. But she hadn't known what it would be like. How *could* she have known all this would happen – the past coming alive again, out of control?

She closed her eyes tightly, as if it would help her hide from what had happened. The worst thought was that maybe she'd *wanted* her mother dead; for she'd certainly gone to extremes to avoid knowing the truth. Surely nothing *more* could happen now. She clung hard to the thought. Perhaps Adam would come back tomorrow, and tell her Jake was safe, and that would be the end of it.

She kept her eyes closed, trying to go to sleep. If she opened them, she wouldn't see anything – once the lights were turned off down here, it was pitch-black. She wasn't afraid of the dark; but now, after a few nights here, she was beginning to admit to herself that she didn't really like such a depth of blackness.

It was out of the blackness that the sea came. Ruth heard it in her sleep at first, a far-off murmur that didn't seem to mean much. But it came close, tugging her back to consciousness; still mostly asleep, she recognized it.

The flood had come. In a short flashing dream she saw green water foaming down the basement stairs. Horrified, she tried to wrench herself from sleep – then the water struck, roaring round her ears. She took in breath to scream, but it had caught her up like a shred of paper.

22

Greenness whirled round her. The walls of the room had disappeared; she was deep in the echoing sea. She struggled, kicking out hopelessly, and her heart almost burst with panic. Drowning! The water clashed in her ears as she went down and down.

Then there was a change, like a snap in her mind, as everything turned quiet and became a dark, easy drifting. She realized her eyes were closed. But there seemed to be a dim edge of light round each eyelid, as if it were not utterly pitch-dark here at the bottom of the sea.

It's a dream, she thought. Either that, or I've drowned.

There was only one sound, a murmurous sighing that might have been her own blood in her ears. She had a feeling of being carried such distances by the water that it was impossible for any more harm to come to her. At last she opened her eyes.

It was a green dark, full of a deep solemn hushing like heartbeats. All around her there were trees – huge, old, their foliage so high that not a leaf was distinguishable. The air that stirred round their trunks seemed green, thick, rippling – as if it were not air but drifting water.

A forest, under the sea? This *must* be a dream. She touched one of the trees, and the grey bark was deeply grooved, rasping her fingers. It felt perilously real.

She began to walk between the vast trunks, into the green dimness. There was no struggle, like trying to walk through water; but she had a sense of floating, as if her body had become insubstantial, like an air bubble. The sighing of the forest came to her dizzily, like sounds

23

heard through water. Was she breathing? She couldn't tell. Oh, *what was happening . . .*?

"Come to the pool, mortal."

She stopped dead. A voice – but it was not a voice, it was a sound like the cry of a seagull, shaped into human words. Ruth found it difficult to move. Then, forcing herself, she stepped towards it.

The trees opened in a glade that collected the shadows like a cup. He was leaning on his spear by a pool, a green cloak drifting round him, a silver helmet on his head, his gaze bent on the dark ring of water. Water, underneath water . . . The spear-tip glimmered, the brightest thing in all the forest. Ruth felt suddenly weak, and went down on her knees in a patch of ferns, facing him across the pool.

He spoke, and his voice seemed to come from very far off. "Do not be afraid. This is the Drowned Forest, which once stood on the land, before the sea came in over it. The trees remember humankind, and will do you no harm."

The Drowned Forest? So she *was* under the sea; this was green water around her, not air. She stared at the warrior in front of her; his helmet was intricately engraved, with sweeping lines and curves that reminded her briefly of Jake's cup. He was, she realized, one of the spearmen from Starr Hills; but close to, he looked slender for a warrior, and was no taller than herself. His face, shadowed under the heavy helm, was fragile as ivory; and silence seemed to wrap him, as if he were deep in a dream.

She whispered, "What did you do to Jake? Did you – kill him?"

"No." It was hard to read his voice; there was no tone in it, only the long lonesome cadence. "We were sent to kill him; but he is one who can pass between the worlds as simply as waking. Our spears never touched him. He fled away into the brightness where we could not follow."

What was that supposed to mean? "What about my brother?" said Ruth tightly. "What happened to him?"

"He is safe too."

Ruth closed her eyes, the weight of relief making her feel how afraid she'd been. I thought they'd been killed, she realized. It never occurred to her to doubt the warrior's word.

Afterwards, she wondered why she hadn't asked more questions (Where are they now? Why did you attack them?); but as she opened her eyes again her whole mind seemed drawn away from such matters, towards the warrior who stood before her. She felt, with a certainty she couldn't explain, that he had called her here, and for some purpose. She said, "Who are you?"

He looked up slowly, with the strange lost gaze she remembered. "I am Fand. Fand the Gentle, the Tear that crosses the light of the eye . . . " He seemed to sigh, and his eyes went starkly up to the spear-point. "But no more. Fand is a warrior now, like all the Women of Fincara."

Women? A shock jarred through Ruth; Fand reached up and, with an effort, pulled off the heavy silver helmet. A cloud of long fair hair spread outwards in the water.

Ruth looked, in silence. A woman warrior. It had been obvious, really; their ghostly slenderness, their voices like wild birds – she had not, she realized, ever thought of them as *men*.

"Come," said Fand, low, "let me tell you why I called you here. We seek Undry, mortal. Have you heard of it, in your world?"

Ruth caught her breath, remembering Jake's message for Adam. "I've – *heard* of it. I don't know what it is."

"It is the Cauldron." Fand left a silence round the words, and all the depths of the sea seemed to gather in stillness. Ruth couldn't have spoken in that moment, even to say she didn't understand.

"Once I was mortal, like you," said Fand – slowly, as if the words came hard. "But I wedded with one of the Undying Ones: Manannan, great Lord of the Sea. When he and his brothers left this world, I could not go with him, but he gave me the gift of never growing old. Immortality he could not give me; one day I will die. Yet I have lived many thousands of years, and am no older now than the day my lord left me. It was a grief, that day – yet soft and easy, beside the griefs I now know."

She paused. And a change seemed to be taking place inside Ruth; she no longer felt stolid and sensible. Fand's words had set her trembling inwardly, like reeds in a sudden strong current. What's *happening* to me? she thought.

Fand spoke again. "After our lords left, I and my sisters went to live on an island here in Undersea. It is not far away; an hour's journey through the Forest would bring us to the shore from which it can be seen. Once it was called Murias, and many stories were told of how it had sunk down from the upper world to Undersea. But now it is called the Isle of Fincara; for we were not left to live

26

there long in peace. The Witch Fincara came."

Shadows were settling thicker, as if great birds had come to perch in the branches overhead. "Who's she?" Ruth asked.

Fand paused, and her eyes looked blind. "You are a mortal; you do not know what witches are. Listen. Otherworld is the half of your world which few mortals enter, for they do not know the way; and it is ruled by powers of light. But the dark powers are always in battle with them, striving to overcome. The Witch Fincara has grown very great amongst them – so great that now she believes she can conquer the guardians of light. They say that once she too was mortal. I do not know; she seems to me to have no human heart left in her."

"What did she do to you?" Ruth asked, her mouth dry.

"She bewitched us." Fand's voice shook, just perceptibly. "We sought only to live our lives, remembering our lords in song and music, and in gentleness to one another. But she would not leave us be. She took our island for herself and made us her warriors. We bear these spears for her; we raid, and maim, and kill, for her..."

The words died in trembling echoes, leaving dark eddies in the water. Ruth wondered how much more of this she could bear.

Almost inaudibly, Fand said, "Look at me, mortal, and you will see the mark of her spell in my face."

Reluctantly, Ruth looked up into the cold changeless eyes. She hadn't thought she would understand what Fand meant; but after only a moment the sense came to her that she was looking at a prisoner – at someone captive, helpless. It was as clear as if bars were there before Fand's face. She stared, her mind in turmoil. She said, desperately, "I still don't see why you called me here."

"The Witch gave us one promise. It was, that when Undry was returned to her, she would have no more need of us, and would set us free. Mortal" – suddenly Fand's voice shook again, wildly – "mortal, though you do not realize it, the Cauldron is very close to you. Open your eyes, and know it!"

Ruth stared, appalled. Me, she thought, find this Cauldron? *How?*

It was quiet in the Forest, the great branches sighing in the drifting currents. Slowly, Fand leaned her forehead on the spear-shaft, fair hair raying out in the water. "I have a great fear," she whispered, more than ever with the voice of a seagull. "It is that Fincara will send me and my sisters into the last battle between the light and the dark; and that we will conquer. Mortal, I could not bear to be the one who slays the light. I beg you to bring her Undry."

By this time Ruth was so shaken, so deeply at a loss, she could have wept. She'd had a dream once in which she'd ceased to be herself, and had to walk amidst crowds of jeering people, asking them who she was. She could never remember how the dream ended. But this felt queerly the same – being called on to do something she knew she couldn't, and by one whose freedom depended on it. Why should Fand *matter* to me? she wondered desperately. Yet looking up, she didn't know how to refuse her.

She looked down again, wearily, at the dark pool between them. Deep in the water the spark of Fand's spear glinted; Ruth reached to touch it, and the reflection broke up in faint rings.

"It is sweet water." Fand's voice was low. "But do not drink, mortal; it is hard for those who drink here to return to their own world ... "

Ruth flinched, taking her hand away. But the silence deepened, and she felt more than ever the changes in her. She couldn't tell why her whole being responded to Fand so urgently; it was as if threads joined their souls, tugging.

Fand whispered, "Long ago I drank from this pool. What I would give to walk free in the mortal world again!"

Blackness was beginning to cloud Ruth's eyes, as if she were fainting. She wondered if Fand had enchanted her, but knew at once the Woman had no such powers. It's something in me, she thought helplessly; something new, something I don't understand, something that just goes out to her.

Darkness whirled round her, and she could hardly see Fand any more; only the spear-tip burned, like a dim flame. But Fand's voice came distantly, tingling with despair. "Help me, mortal! Bring Undry!"

Ruth reached out urgently, wanting all at once to grip her hand. "Yes!" she cried. "*I promise ... *"

Darkness came down completely. Ruth heard the trees moan as the black flood swelled, sweeping her away till she knew no more.

Chapter 3

"Here, have another cup o' coffee," Gran said, pouring it out. "Happen it'll wake you up. Are you not well, lovey? I had a rare job rousing you this morning."

Ruth treated herself to sugar in the coffee. It was ten o'clock, the time when she and Gran could sit down after clearing away the breakfasts. Usually she was well awake by now, but today she felt dazed and exhausted, dragged from sleep as if from drowning.

"Sorry," she said. "I had a weird dream. I suppose I didn't sleep properly till morning. I'll feel better once I'm outside, I think. Is there much shopping to do?"

"Nay, I'll see to the shopping," said Gran. "I've to go out anyway. You have a sit down, love, you look peaky to me. I can get the beds done when I'm back."

Ruth felt guilty; Gran wasn't paying her to sit down. "I'm all right — " she began, but to her horror had to stop short. Oh *no* . . . what on earth was there to cry for?

Gran sighed. "Now then," she said helplessly. "Drink up your coffee, love. It'll be me carrying on about your mother that's done this. But you've no call to lose sleep and take on about her."

Her mother . . . She'd almost forgotten – almost

forgotten everything except Fand. But there was Jake too, and Adam, and her mother . . .

She leaned her head in her hands. There was too much going on for just one person to deal with. "Gran," she said, "what was the story you used to tell Adam about our mother?"

Gran drew in her breath. "Nay, love. It was nowt but nonsense about how she looked, and the songs she sang, and that sort o' stuff. Best forgotten . . . "

Her voice seemed to fray with foreboding; it was as if, Ruth thought, Gran had forbidden herself to speak. And did she, herself, really want to hear? But why should she be afraid of hearing about her own mother?

"I'm not a kid, Gran," she said. "You – didn't like her, did you?"

Gran sighed, defeated. "No. I didn't and that's truth. I had a horror of her. Times I'd lie in my bed, late at night, and shudder to think my Jake'd wedded her in a Christian church."

A coldness stole over Ruth – inexplicably familiar, like a half-stirred memory. But that was stupid; she'd been much too young, when her mother left, to remember anything about her.

Gran said, "She had a lovely face, and hair as fair as a babby's, long enough to sit on. But I could never take to her. She had a way of laughing, and singing, and it was like ice down your back. I kept out of her way. But she witched Jake. He papered this room for her – red roses for love, he said . . . "

For as long as Ruth could remember, huge red roses had sprawled across the kitchen walls, fading gradually

31

to a sandy brown against the yellowed background. Her eyes stung, as if she might cry again. Red roses for love . . . it seemed so like Jake.

"I've ne'er been as glad of anything as when she went," Gran said, harshly. "He was never steady in his mind, Jake. There's a fault in our family – they say it shows itself once each generation. I always thought, if he marries a good girl, it'll maybe settle him. But she turned his wits beyond help."

Ruth didn't look up at her; she could guess the burning look of pain, bitterness. It was an old story that Jake and Sarah's father had never married Gran – afraid, perhaps, of the sort of children a Demdyke would bear.

"And so she went," said Gran, wearily. "I allus knew she would, some time; when she felt she'd done my Jake enough harm. I've turned it over and over in my mind, and it seems to me – I ne'er told the lad this, lovey – but it seems to me she waited till she'd borne my Jake a son in his own image, as if she knew that'd grieve him as nothing else could. The lad's Jake, every inch; it turns my heart over, times, to see him. And I can all but hear her laugh in my ears, too. 'He's your picture, Jake,' she used to say over the laddie's cot, laughing like a witch; and I could've killed her for it."

Ruth took a drink of hot coffee. She felt cold.

"She never knew", said Gran, "that Jake'd leave him to come looking for her, and ne'er see him grown. It was my heart that broke when he went, yet I never had him searched for; I dursn't think what'd come, if he saw the lad now."

32

Ruth shivered. Jake had seen Adam; and what would come from it, heaven only knew.

Gran laid her hand over Ruth's. "There now. You're right to say you're no babby, lass. I only pray you can bear what I've told you like a grown girl, and have sense. I could've told it no different."

Ruth wondered what she'd expected to be told. That her mother was just an ordinary woman, charmed at first by Jake's queer ways, but then growing bored and leaving him? Nothing so commonplace could happen to the crazy Demdykes. "I had to know, didn't I?" she said, making her voice come out firm. "It's all right, Gran. I feel better now, actually."

That was a lie. But Gran accepted it, patting her hand and then looking round at the clock as if to remind herself life had to go on.

"Eh, is that the time?" she said sharply. "I've to see them at the bank shortly – there's that guttering to be fixed, and no money for it wi'out they'll give me a loan."

It was a relief to turn to something so mundane. "The guttering?" said Ruth. "What's wrong with it?"

"It's rusted through," said Gran, in disgust. "I thought it'd last another year, but wi' the rain this summer I shall have to get it fixed. And it's criminal what they charge, for that new plastic doings. All these prices go up faster than I can shame to put up the rents . . . " She got up, stiffly. "There's coffee still warm in the pot, love, so don't stir till you've a mind. And don't fret, you hear me? Else I shall ne'er forgive myself."

Ruth made herself smile. "I won't, Gran, honestly."

"That's my lass. And don't fret about your brother, neither. He's gone off after your dad before, times out of mind – but two–three days and he's allus home again, wanting fed."

At least she knew Adam was safe now. "All right, Gran," she said; and Gran put on her hat and coat and departed, leaving Ruth on her own.

The house was empty and quiet, all the guests having left for the day. For once, sunshine was slanting in; and Ruth sat at the table, drawing with her finger round the shadow of the coffee cup – then abruptly got up, opened the basement door and went down the steps into the darkness.

There was a window in her bedroom, but it just looked on to a tiny area and didn't let in much light. She sat down on her bed and, without knowing why, reached for Jake's cup.

Why hadn't she been *glad* to hear her mother was still alive? That would have been normal, surely; more normal than this chill she felt. There must be something in me that remembers her, Ruth thought; it can't be a total blank. Maybe if I try, something'll come back.

She wasn't sure she wanted to try. It was beginning to be clear there was something fearful about her mother. But I can't go on like this, she thought; I'll be scared of my own shadow soon! Whatever Gran says about her, she's only a woman, not some sort of witch. If I could just remember her, as she was, that might be one thing less to be scared about.

Holding the cup, she closed her eyes. The earliest thing

34

she could remember was sitting on a pink-and-grey rug in the kitchen; it was a memory that often drifted into her mind, vague and unsummoned, just before she fell asleep. She knew it came from far back, because she felt so tiny on the rug, looking up at huge shapes.

It was a faint memory, usually; more of a dim sensation than a picture, sliding imperceptibly into sleep. But as Ruth concentrated, gripping the cup, it began to clear, colours emerging. Red roses, giant-size, spread over the walls. An old rocking chair, where Jake had always sat, stood like a cliff. The memory seemed to grow strongly into life, much more real than the present moment; the glossy cream-coloured cooker stood like a house, black knobs winking like eyes, and the big brown table *was* a house, roofed over and four-square. That cooker had gone now, and the table had been moved down into the basement . . .

A sound entered the picture, clear and pure as birdsong. Somebody singing . . . but the small Ruth, looking up from the rug, didn't like it; the clear trickling notes were like a shiver down her back, like raindrops sliding down a windowpane. She could feel her face puckering, about to cry.

Something stirred by the window. Something as tall as a steeple, in a trailing black dress, fair hair cascading; a face turned, looking down at Ruth, with long mocking green eyes that glimmered like the sea. They saw Ruth's crumpling face, and at once the lips curved upward, laughing, and sang louder. Stooping, long white hands on knees, the woman sang tauntingly down at her.

35

From thy mother, in Undersea,
Witch's power comes to thee.
But you'll never know, my child,
Never know, my silly daughter,
How to work the magic wild
Of Undersea, of underwater.
This my spell on you is laid:
You'll be always too afraid.

Ruth wrenched her eyes open, starting to her feet, gripping the metal cup so hard it hurt. Gasping for breath, she stared wildly round to convince herself of where she was. Her mother. She'd remembered her mother. Tall and fair, green eyes full of glimmers – and the laughing, the singing like ice down her back. It was all true. Everything Gran said had been true.

The song lilted on and on in her head – an Undersea song, unearthly as the Drowned Forest in its green waters. *Was* her mother some sort of witch, trying to lay spells? And what had she to do with Undersea? I don't understand, Ruth thought, and felt tears bead her eyelashes. Oh, if only she could stop *crying* . . .

Upstairs a door slammed. Then a voice shouted, hoarsely, "Hey! Anybody home?"

Ruth stood, numbly, holding the cup. Still her mother's voice lilted wickedly in her head, and unseen waters seemed to shift coldly round her. *From thy mother, in Undersea . . .*

"For Christ's sake! *Is anyone home?*"

Adam was back.

*

He was leaning against the back door where he'd slammed it – filthy, crumpled, and pale with hunger. But as Ruth came out of the basement, all she was struck by, quite irrelevantly, was his likeness to Jake; for an instant she almost thought it *was* Jake, standing there. Then as she stared, she saw the glittering violence in his eyes, in place of Jake's gentleness. It was queer, that difference. In the ordinary daylight Adam looked fiercer, wilder, than he had on Starr Hills. Madder, Ruth thought bluntly. Madder even than Jake.

She took a grip on herself, thrusting away her stupid weepiness. She would need to be extra sensible and down-to-earth to cope with Adam now. "I suppose you want something to eat," she said.

He stared at her, eyes shifting to what she held in her hands. Ruth realized she was still carrying Jake's cup. Heaven knew why; and the ridiculous notion crossed her mind that the cup itself had wanted her to. *Stop it*, she thought.

"Give it here!" Adam flung himself at her, furiously snatching it. "He came – and I hadn't got it to give him!"

Ruth stiffened, afraid his fists might fly in her direction. "Sit down," she said, keeping her voice calm, "and I'll make you breakfast."

He stood glowering at her dangerously; then abruptly shoved the cup on to the windowsill, among some geraniums that stood there in pots, and sat down at the table. "Don't ever touch it again," he said between his teeth.

He was like a bad gangster movie; laughable if she'd felt like laughing. Which she didn't. Adam was so *extreme*; they really would cart him off to a padded cell one of these days. Without answering, she got out the frying pan and began to do him bacon and eggs. The familiar task reassured her, and after a moment she said quietly, "What happened to you?"

He looked at her from under his brows. "I don't know," he said sullenly. "I must have passed out. Where did you go?"

"I looked for you, but I couldn't find you. I came home," Ruth said. She gave him the bacon and eggs and he set to ravenously. Ruth poured herself another cup of coffee and sat down facing him; then said, deliberately, "I saw those people with spears as well."

Adam went utterly still, staring at her as if time had stopped. At last he said hoarsely, "What else did you see?"

"Jake," said Ruth. "Listen, Adam. He gave me a message for you. He said – *Tell him Undry must be returned.*"

His brows creased slowly. "What does that mean?" he said.

"Don't you know?"

"No." He sighed, and looked broodingly at nothing. "I sometimes wonder who's crazier, him or me."

Ruth began to relax; she could never be certain of him, but his violent mood seemed over now. "You're *not* crazy," she told him. "But honestly, Adam, you don't help yourself."

His lips tightened. "I know."

Ruth was used to feeling afraid in his presence; but now the fear that touched her seemed more on his account than on her own. "Adam," she said, "what's *wrong?*"

"I dunno." He didn't look up. "I – I'm like an actor without any lines. That's the only way I've ever found to describe it. I'm up on a stage, with a play going on all round me, but no one's given me a script and I don't know what to say or do. Sometimes I try to make it up, but it never works." He looked at her, dark eyes desperate. "I get scared, and then I get angry. I'm sorry I yelled at you, Ruth."

Ruth was silent. The words had an unlocked sound, tumbling out as if he'd never dared say them before. She felt deeply moved by this picture of his plight; it exactly expressed how hard he was to understand, how hard just to talk to. But if he can see himself so clearly, she thought, he can't be crazy. What *is* wrong with him?

She said, "Some day you'll find your script."

"Maybe. But I think I've got to find Jake first. And Fincara."

It was like having the breath knocked out of her. "*Who?*"

Adam stared, surprised. "Fincara. Our mother."

It was as if he really had struck her, then. Ruth almost thought she lost consciousness; a queer ringing dark seemed to descend. When her sight cleared, she saw Adam on his feet, off balance, as if he'd started round the table towards her.

"Who did you say?" she whispered, lips stiff. "*Fincara . . . ?*"

"Yes," said Adam tautly. "What's wrong, had you forgotten her name? Our own mother?"

It was as if her sight hadn't totally cleared; the currents of Undersea seemed to move round her, and somewhere Fand watched her silently, eyes full of darkness. "Oh, leave me alone," she whispered, scarcely knowing what she said. "Leave me alone, Adam ... "

She told herself later that she couldn't have been expected to remember what a knife-edge he lived on, how hard it was for him to trust anyone. She didn't see his face change, eyes lighting with anger, rejection; the first she knew was when he knocked his plate crashing across the room and yelled, "To hell with you, then!" He turned, and went clattering down the stairs into the basement, slamming the door behind him.

She didn't know how long she sat at the table, letting her coffee go cold. It seemed years, ages later when she found herself picking up pieces of broken plate and wiping fried egg off the tiles – so that Gran, when she returned, would find the kitchen tidy.

Chapter 4

Ruth pulled the coverlet straight over the bed in No. 4. Doing the rooms in the morning fell into an easy rhythm – make the bed, tidy up anything the guests had left around, dust the tops, wash up the teacups if they'd been used, clean the washbasin, put out fresh teabags and sachets of coffee, sugar and milk powder, then go round with the Hoover. She never minded housework. Jenny said she was appallingly unliberated.

But it helped her to stop thinking. And she needed that sort of help; because although nothing had happened in the four days since Adam had returned from Starr Hills, the nights were becoming more than she could bear. She dreamt again and again of Fincara – the taunting song, the green eyes full of cold laughter – and woke sweating. There was nothing she could do about it. She couldn't ask Aunt Sarah or Uncle Nick to help; there was no way of explaining it to them without sounding crazy.

She hadn't touched Jake's cup again; it remained on the kitchen windowsill, a potent reminder of everything that was wrong. Gran had noticed it three evenings ago, when they were getting the breakfast things ready, and had pushed it behind one of the geraniums as if she didn't like the sight of it. "Eh, has that turned up again?" Ruth had heard her mutter. "It'll be that lad, hunting through Jake's stuff the way he does..." Clearly, she didn't remember Jake had given it to Ruth, and Ruth said nothing; she didn't want to talk about it.

"Ruth, lovey, are you there?"

It was Gran's voice from the bottom of the stairs. She was calling quietly, in case there were any guests still around to be disturbed; she couldn't easily climb the stairs, because of her rheumatism. Ruth went out and ran down to her. "Yes, Gran?"

"Ben Hesketh'll be coming to collect them boxes this afternoon, lovey. I'll need your brother to help carry 'em up. Can you fetch him? He'll be at Starr Hills, I daresay."

Gran had been refused a bank loan for new guttering – because of her age, she opined huffily – so had decided to sell off some possessions that had come to her from her mother. Ben Hesketh, an antique dealer, was a friend of Jake's whom Ruth remembered from the old days – Jake's only friend, really. He had left them two small crates, and yesterday Ruth had helped Gran pack up her lovely old china – fragile blue-and-white majolica ware, Staffordshire teapots and Bristol figures, mostly chipped or cracked, but still beautiful. The packing had been done in the basement to avoid breakages, and the two crates stood at the foot of the stairs. They were heavy, and Ben Hesketh would need help to carry them out to his car. But... she'd hardly spoken to Adam since the morning he'd returned from Starr Hills. His white face, his

42

burning eyes, the sense of barely suppressed violence about him, warned her to keep her distance.

"I can help Mr Hesketh, Gran," she said.

"Nay, I know lasses do all that lads do nowadays, but them boxes weigh heavy. 'Twon't hurt the lad to help once in a while. I get no other work out of him."

"I don't think he's – quite well, Gran."

Gran sighed. "It's his father in him. Take no heed, lass. There was never owt to be done with Jake when he took on that wild-eyed look."

Ruth felt cold. It seemed Gran too sensed there was no way of stopping whatever it was that had begun . . . "I'll fetch him when I've finished the bedrooms," she said.

She set off about an hour later, the pockets of her waterproof stocked with chocolate bars against starvation. Crossing the coast road, she climbed up the gradual grassy slope on the landward side of the sea wall. A promenade ran along the top, and Ruth saw Council workmen piling sandbags against the brightly painted railings. So this talk of a flood was getting serious . . .

She walked along the promenade towards Starr Hills. There wasn't much to look at, though for once the sky was clear; gulls were drifting round and round in an uneasy crowd, hardly making a sound, like scraps of newspaper spiralling in the wind. The tide was advancing, but there was still a bleak expanse of mud flats left uncovered beyond the beach. The beach itself was all stones.

Ruth wondered why people still came to Wickrithe for their holidays. Habit, Gran said dryly, when asked; and Ruth knew she got fewer bookings every year. Old people

43

still came, liking the quietness and the fact that there were no hills to climb; but there's absolutely nothing to do, Ruth thought, except go for gentle walks along the promenade, or – if you're feeling really energetic – play a game of bowls in the park.

It hadn't always been so. Gran said that once Wickrithe had been all golden sands. Even I can remember there used to be a narrow strip of sand, winding along between the stones, Ruth thought; it wasn't a total waste of time, bringing our buckets and spades here when we were kids. Except that we preferred Starr Hills ... She could remember the old pier, too – falling down by then, too unsafe for anyone to be allowed on it – but in Gran's day bustling and lively with peepshows, a funfair, and a small steam railway running the entire length. Right at the end a glass pavilion had been built for concerts and parties, and Gran said people had come from as far away as Lancaster.

But the best thing I can remember, Ruth thought, is the swingboats. She'd never seen swings like them before or since – wooden boats painted bright yellow with curlicues of red and green, where two of you sat facing each other and pulled alternately on ropes to swing yourselves higher and higher. It had made the day perfect when Gran paid for her and Adam to have a ride; she could still remember the glorious whoosh to and fro, the sense of riding in the air like the wheeling gulls, the bitter disappointment when the woman in charge came to catch their swingboat and tell them their time was up. Adam had often refused to get out, and Gran had had to pay for another ride.

Things had changed since then. The swings had gone and the pier had been demolished; a few years ago the Council had given permission for a café-and-restaurant to be built, but the place had only been open a month when it caught fire and was burned out; the Fire Brigade couldn't get to it, the promenade being too narrow for their vehicles. The gutted remains were still there, blackened and dismal.

Otherwise there was just the mud, and the stones. Wickrithe was old – mentioned in the Domesday Book, Ruth had heard – and before seaside holidays were invented, the shore would have been busy with fishing boats. Now it was empty as it couldn't have been for centuries, left to the tide and the seabirds.

A mist began to roll in off the sea; and suddenly, before Ruth really noticed what was happening, everything beyond ten yards was blotted out. It seemed typical of Wickrithe, to produce a fog on the only day this week it hadn't rained. After a while, though, dismissing her memories, Ruth began to like it; the sun was behind the mist, turning it into a glimmery silver haze; and at least it was a different sort of weather. She walked on until she reached Starr Hills. The sea wall ended, steps going down from the promenade and burying themselves in sand. Ruth went down, then climbed up again into the dunes, wondering how she was going to find Adam.

It felt warm; the sun was a raying gold core in the mist, and she could smell heath grass and flowers – vetch, trefoil, loosestrife, campion. In the quietness seagulls called far above her, invisible and lonesome. And then she saw Adam.

He was down on the shore, a shadow edged with silver light, combing the tideline. Ruth stood watching him. Sometimes he picked something up, squatting on heels to examine it, then slipped it into a bag that hung from his shoulder; or put it down again, going on. The tide was close in by now, and his footprints behind him filled up with water, gleaming.

I don't feel afraid of him any more, Ruth thought, curiously. Or of anything. The mist, blotting out Wick-rithe, seemed to banish her tension and sense of danger; she and Adam were alone and safe, as they'd always been on Starr Hills.

"Adam!" she called.

He looked up and saw her. She climbed down the dune and walked towards him. Hitching the bag up on his shoulder, he came to meet her. "Hullo," he said.

Close to, he looked less mad than he had done for ages; just drawn, pale, weary. He and Jake always look as if they've got one skin less than other people, Ruth thought. It's that, really, that makes people call them crazy.

"Hullo," she said. "What are you doing?"

"Picking things up. There's a man who runs a jewellery-making class at the tech – he pays me for stones they can use." He dug a hand into his bag and brought it out to show Ruth. "See?"

It was a handful of small pebbles, veined with amber, green, cobalt. Shaped and polished, they would wink like jewels.

"That's lovely," Ruth said, picking out from amongst them a spiral shell, cream and pink with an almost pearly translucence. It looked as if it should have broken, amongst the pebbles in Adam's bag.

"They'll give me fifty pence for that at the souvenir shop," Adam said. "And then charge some townie a couple of quid for it." He hesitated. "Have it, if you like. I can find others."

Ruth looked at him surprised. "Are you sure?"

" 'Course. Have you got anything to eat? I haven't had any lunch."

Ruth put the shell away in the safest pocket of her waterproof, and gave him one of the chocolate bars. They sat on the soft sand above the tideline while Adam ate; there had always been fewer stones here, on this remote end of the beach where hardly anyone came. The mist was thicker, closing them inside a shining globe. It's like being all alone in our own world, Ruth thought. She wanted to stay, basking in this unexpected sense of peace.

"They're sandbagging the railings on the promenade," she said. "Is there really going to be a flood, d'you think?"

"Depends," said Adam through a mouthful of chocolate. "It isn't the rain here that counts, it's the rain up on the hills where the river starts. It used not to matter, because they dredged a deep-water channel from Emmerton to here, to let the ships get through to the port. But they stopped doing that last year."

"Why?" Ruth asked idly. Emmerton was the commercial port upriver, the nearest large town to Wickrithe.

"The port closed. It'd been running at a loss for years. It

was their job to dredge the channel, so it's not being done any more."

"So the channel's silting up?"

Adam nodded. "Yes. If there's a lot of heavy rain on the hills, and more water than usual comes down, it could overflow the banks."

"It'll be safe enough if they sandbag the whole of the promenade, though, won't it?" Ruth asked.

"Won't make any difference," said Adam rather scornfully. "Don't you remember the Liggard Brook? Runs into the river by Copers Bakery? The floodwater'll just go right up there and spread out over the town. Or come in over Starr Hills and do the same."

Copers Bakery was upriver, at the other end of the sea wall; Ruth could remember the deep channel of the Liggard Brook running past. It didn't sound too hopeful. "Isn't the sea wall any use, then?" she said.

"It was OK when the river was dredged. It protected the town against high tides then. But it's no use against flood-water coming downstream."

"Great," said Ruth. "I really don't fancy the thought of a flood."

"Don't you?" said Adam without expression. He stared out to sea, crumpling the chocolate wrapper slowly in his hand. "I do. I'd like to see this bloody place sunk right down under the sea."

His sudden swings of mood always seemed to catch Ruth off her guard. "You don't mean that," she said after a moment, lamely. "You ought to stop brooding so much about our parents, Adam . . . "

Adam's arm went back, and he flung the crumpled wrapper violently into the sea. "Shut up! You saw Jake, and those people with spears – that wasn't *brooding*! That was *real*!"

Ruth bit her lip. Giving Adam the chocolate bar, letting him tell her those rather dull facts about the sea defences, it had been so easy to forget what was going on – to feel he was just her little brother and everything was ordinary, normal. But she knew now that he lived in a state near total despair, his life so meaningless he didn't know how to live it, his one certainty that he had to find Jake and Fincara. Remembering all that put an end to her peace.

She leaned forward, hugging her knees. Safely enclosed in the shining mist, it was after all quite easy to speak. "Adam. I've got a lot more to tell you, if you'll listen."

"What?" he said wearily.

Ruth began to tell him her dream of Fand, the Drowned Forest, and the Isle of Fincara under the sea. As she'd half expected, his face cleared slowly as she spoke, dark eyes lighting up with an almost painful eagerness.

"Yes," he said under his breath as she finished, "I've dreamed about that Drowned Forest too. And I've dreamed about an island, with a castle; and another forest, on the land, with huge great oaks and lots of lakes and streams. It's like I'm only ever really alive in those dreams."

Poor Adam . . . "I was afraid, in the Drowned Forest," Ruth said.

"You needn't be," said Adam, with certainty. "It's real. It was all forest here once, and then, ages ago, there was a flood; the forest sank down under the sea. Lots of the trees are still down there in the estuary. They used to be fetched up when the channel was being dredged, and drift ashore. Don't you remember those massive tree trunks we used to see, all along the beach?"

Ruth remembered. The great skeletal tree trunks, sun-warmed on the sand – she and Adam had climbed on them, scrambling over the huge crooked shapes. She looked out to sea, as far as she could through the mist, and thought of great trees whispering under the waves. "Yes; I remember," she said.

"I wish you were here more often," said Adam. "I can talk to you."

Ruth looked at him, surprised. "You haven't, much."

"More than I have to anyone else. Usually I keep quiet in case people think I'm crazy. Look – what it comes down to is, Jake and Fand both want this Undry thing. But how do we find it? What is it?"

"The Cauldron, Fand called it," Ruth said.

"H'm." Adam frowned thoughtfully; then his eyes widened, and he pointed a finger at Ruth. "The cup!"

"That old thing? That's not a *cauldron*."

"It must be. That's what Jake came for, the first time. He told me to fetch it. And you know where he got it from, don't you?"

"No . . ."

"He got it from Fincara! She left it behind when she went away. That was when he gave it to you."

50

Ruth seemed to lose her breath, as if she'd been punched. From *Fincara* . . . That cup, which she'd carried round with her for years, touched, held – it had come from Fincara, out of those cold white hands!

"Adam," she said, lips stiff, "Fincara's the witch Fand talked about."

Adam frowned. "I don't see why she should call her a witch. But everyone's always been frightened of Fincara. Gran is. And none of those bloody people in Wickrithe ever talk about her, except behind our backs . . . "

"Anyway," Ruth said, "it's her Fand wants Undry for."

"I suppose so."

"So how does Jake come into it? Why does he want it too?"

Adam was silent, his frown deepening. Then he said flatly, "He can't want it for Fincara, because Fand attacked him. So they must be on different sides."

And I promised Fand to give Undry to Fincara, so I'm on her side, Ruth thought. It was like ice inside her. "Does Jake want it just to stop Fincara from getting it?" she said. "What did he say, when he asked you to bring it to him?"

"Nothing anyone could understand. He said, 'I must return it to the half-mortals, for only they in all the worlds can keep it safe now.' "

Ruth was silent, baffled. She could almost hear Jake saying the words, full of soft urgency; but what did they mean?

"What do we do now, then?" said Adam.

The mist shone round them, shutting out the world. As Ruth tried to find an answer, a faint lost crying sounded far above, like seagulls. A great jolt of dismay went through her; and almost before she understood why, spear-points came stabbing through the mist, bright-bladed. A cold clear voice echoed, vengeful as a gull's scream: "Now you pay your debt to the sea, mortals!"

Shapes wreathed out of the mist, coming from the dunes; Ruth saw a green trail of cloaks, light striking from silver helmets, and a cold transfixing stare. She scrambled to her feet, clutching at Adam's arm, and Fincara's Women advanced in a semicircle, the mist rolling with them. The spear-points, burning, reached out.

"Get back!" Adam gasped. He seized Ruth's shoulder, jerking her violently back from the spears; and, stumbling, she felt the sea lap round her ankles.

The spears followed, each tip sparked with flame. Panting, Ruth looked desperately round at the great host of Women. Their voices were rising in a long, edged, lifting cry like seagulls before a storm. "Fand!" she cried.

There was no reply. Still the spears came on, forcing them step by step into the sea, till they were almost knee-deep. Ruth wanted to turn and plunge away, to strike out blindly through the water; but Adam kept hold of her, and she knew the coast here was treacherous – even at full tide there were currents that could sweep you out to sea.

Then Adam stopped, flinging up an arm to ward off the blades. "What do you want?" he shouted.

52

The spears paused fractionally. Then a voice rang out, bitter as death: "What your sister promised, mortal! Now drown!"

The spears leapt forward. Ruth heard herself scream as Adam lost his grip on her, and she fell down into the water. She glimpsed a spear-blade thrusting straight at her face, too fast to dodge, its edge glinting . . .

It was as she'd always imagined being shot, a crash between her eyes. The clamour of gulls' voices rose to a shriek and, with her ears full of it, Ruth fell and fell.

Chapter 5

It was utterly quiet, except for the blood pounding in her ears. There seemed to be a weight on her chest, pinning her to the ground and not letting her breathe. With a tremendous effort Ruth forced her eyes open.

She saw Adam. He was kneeling by a pool, looking up at the towering trees that surrounded him – quiet, intent, somehow unsurprised. Ruth knew there was something strange about him, but it seemed to take her an age to work out what it was: he was wearing a green cloak, and its folds drifted round him as if floating in water. His hair floated too.

An arm was slipped under her shoulders, lifting her; then something was wrapped round her and fastened at the throat. All at once she could breathe again. Her sight cleared slowly, and she saw she too wore a green cloak. She lifted a hand to touch it, thin and silken; then looked up at Fand.

The Woman knelt by her, face shadowed under the heavy helm. Her lips were set and still, like those of a warrior counting his losses after battle.

"It is one of the Sea People's cloaks." Her voice was dull, distant. "A strong charm is woven into it, mortal.

Now you will breathe sea-water and walk without struggle in the land Undersea."

Ruth looked round, her heart beating hard. The tall trees stood, marching away into the green darkness. Far above she could hear the leaves whispering in the currents of Undersea. She could imagine fish creeping amongst those high branches, like birds.

Gritting her teeth, she got up and stood looking around. She was alive; and she'd been here before, in this shadowy glade with the dark pool. But this time it wasn't a dream – she was really here, breathing the drifting green atmosphere as if it were ordinary air. She looked at Adam and saw the mark of the spear between his eyes; blood had flowed, streaking his face. It seemed the water of Undersea didn't mingle with it or wash it away. She touched her own brow, and there was blood there too. The cut wasn't deep; but her mind felt cleaved, riven away from the world she knew.

Adam said, "There's water here, if you're thirsty."

Ruth looked down at the pool, remembering its silken coolness; then a pang of horror came. "No! Adam, you mustn't drink from there!"

"Why not?" said Adam, rising. "I have before."

Ruth stared at him, remembering Fand's words – *It is hard for those who drink here to return to their own world* ... And standing there in his green cloak, Adam looked different from before.

"When?" she whispered.

"Every time I dreamed of this place," Adam said. In the shadowy glade, his eyes seemed piercingly clear. "I was always thirsty, in the dreams. This water was the freshest I

55

ever tasted. After I woke up, it was days before I needed to eat or drink anything again."

"But those were only dreams!"

"Yes. This was the first real time." Adam touched his lips, wonderingly. "I don't feel as if I'll ever be thirsty again."

Ruth's heart went cold. "Oh, Fand, why didn't you stop him?"

Fand rose slowly, setting the butt of her spear on the mossy ground. "I was not present in your brother's dreams, mortal. To dream of drinking from the pool, even though it be only a dream, is to turn one's face away from what mortals call the real world. He was bound to come here and seek to drink in truth. And why should I prevent him?" The white hands tightened, hard, on the spear. "To please you, mortal – who promised me help, and then forgot me?"

That promise, made in a dream . . . "I didn't forget!" Ruth said urgently. "I just didn't know until now that the cup is Undry, Fand!"

"Am I to believe that?" Fand lifted her face, bleak with betrayal. "For seven years you have borne Undry by your side; since you left me, you have held it in your hands. That you of all beings should prate of not knowing!"

The accusation took Ruth's breath away. What did Fand mean, *you of all beings*? "Please Fand – I *didn't* know. Adam, tell her . . . "

"I don't know what she's talking about," said Adam indifferently. Ruth looked round at him, half afraid at his tone.

It wasn't just her imagination; he did look different – taller, straighter. With the green cloak hiding his old

56

clothes, he didn't look like her brother any more, or indeed like anyone from her own world. A prince, she thought crazily, returning to his kingdom . . . Her heart felt cold and heavy again. On Starr Hills, she'd been able to talk to him; but she didn't think she could now.

"Well," said Adam, glancing at Fand, "what are we here for? We haven't got Undry with us, you know."

"You are to go to Fincara. She awaits you in Caer Wydyr, the Glass Castle which she has raised on her isle. Do not try to escape, mortals; for see, the Women surround you."

As if at a signal, nine silver-helmed figures stepped from the forest and stood round the edge of the glade, spears glinting in the gloom. Ruth's heart jumped; escape was precisely what she'd thought of, at the mere mention of Fincara. She looked into the forest to see if the rest of the Women were close enough to catch her, if she could evade these few . . .

"There are no others, mortal." Fand watched her, reading her thoughts. "At need, enchantment can make us seem a host to human eyes; but in truth, there is only myself and my nine companions. Yet our strength is more than an army's. You are our prisoners. Beware."

"I'm not anyone's prisoner!" said Adam sharply. Ruth looked at him despairingly; 'prince' came to her mind again, for he seemed almost arrogantly unafraid. The green currents lifted his hair, revealing the blood on his brow. "I'm Fincara's son," said Adam. "Take me to her."

Ruth couldn't bear any more. "Oh *please*, Fand – don't!"

Fand looked at her; and Adam turned away, as if this

was no concern of his. The other Women bowed their heads, and the silence lengthened, broken only by the murmuring of the huge trees. It was as if Ruth and Fand were once more alone in the little glade.

"Please, Fand," Ruth said – ashamed of herself, but there was nothing she could do about it. "I can't face Fincara."

Fand sighed. "I know, mortal," she said, low as a breath. "But she commands me; I cannot help but do her bidding. Would you had brought Undry to me as I asked you! We would have been spared this!"

"But I didn't know it was Undry," Ruth said desperately. "Truly, Fand."

Fand looked her in the eyes for a long moment; and it was difficult for Ruth to face the utter loneliness of that gaze. But at last Fand nodded slowly. "Yes – it is hard to come to wisdom in the world of humankind." Her voice was achingly bleak. "Now we must all suffer. But perhaps, when Undry is returned, all will be well."

Her voice held no hope, even in those last words. Ruth's thoughts flinched from what it must feel like to be Fand – she seemed hardly to exist, so much had been taken from her.

Another Woman spoke, toneless and distant. "Do not ask us to release you, mortal. We must obey Fincara; we are spellbound. We would die if we tried to break free of the spell – or if we did not, she would come and kill us."

Ruth looked at the ground, pulling the cloak round her to stop a shiver. So that was that, really. If she couldn't help being a coward, at least she could try not to let it show.

Adam stirred impatiently, the green currents eddying round him. "Are you ready to go now?" he said, his voice sounding deep and harsh after the Women's frail tones.

"Yes," said Fand. "Come." She led the way into the forest, and Adam strode after her.

The path was narrow, winding mossily amongst the trees. A feathery grass grew at its edge, swaying in the currents of Undersea; and Ruth, walking behind Adam, saw white anemones opening here and there like small stars. The nine Women came behind her, their footfalls as light as birds'. Almost at once Ruth felt as if she were sliding into a dream; the glade vanished behind them, and soon she seemed to have been walking this path all her life, through the vista of trees, with the tip of Fand's spear faintly gleaming, and Adam ahead of her, treading like a king. Past and future melted away; perhaps I'll wake up, she thought, the way I did before. But at last, all but imperceptibly, the gloom began to lighten ahead.

They came out of the forest into an emptiness where the Undersea currents seemed to drift on and on and up and up for ever. Tilting her head back, Ruth saw that at the farthest height the green melted into a silveriness which, she supposed, was the nearest Undersea got to a sky. Then, looking down again, she stared. At their feet a grassy bank shelved to white sand, and a river the colour of emeralds streamed by.

A river, under the sea. The opposite bank showed dim

as a cloud, two miles away or more. All the green of Undersea seemed to have fused in that clearest of emeralds; it was as different from the drifting atmosphere as, in Ruth's own world, water from air.

"Look not too long, mortal." It was Fand's voice, low and warning. "This river flows out of Annuvin; it will steal the souls of those who gaze unguarded."

With an effort, Ruth raised her eyes from the river; she felt half drowned in it already. "Have we got to cross it?"

"We go only halfway over." Fand pointed. "There lies Fincara's Isle."

Ruth had to force herself to look. The Isle lay about a mile away, in the middle of the river. The green currents drifted densely round it, so that it seemed a floating shadow. Ruth saw it was high on the downriver side, castled with a great crag that fell sheer down to the water; the stone had a dark gleam, like opaque crystal, and was seamed with fissures where she guessed grass and ferns would cling. Below the crag the lie of the land seemed gentler, with the bowed heads of willow trees. The silver thread of a stream ran down to a crescent-shaped beach. But Ruth's eye was drawn back to the great tower of rock, and on the very top, high above, she seemed to see a jut of walls and pinnacles, glimmering like hard edges of light.

"That is Caer Wydyr – the Castle of Glass," said Fand, and the words shed a cold silence. "There Fincara awaits you."

Ruth looked at Adam. He seemed no longer even aware of her, his gaze fixed eagerly on the Isle. She noticed he wasn't peering, eyes wrinkled, as she had – just gazing, as if he could easily see through the dense Undersea drift. As if he's used to it; as if he's in his own world, Ruth thought.

"Well?" he said impatiently. "Let's go, then."

There was a boat drawn up on the shore, dark oak painted white to the waterline, the prow a swan's head. There were five rowing benches, the oars shipped. Adam climbed in and went to stand in the prow, eyes fixed once more on the island. Ruth clenched her hands inside her cloak, nerving herself to follow him; but it was Fand who didn't move. Gripping her spear in white hands, she stood gazing at the shadowy Isle.

At last the Woman who had spoken before said, "Come, Fand,"

Fand's hands tightened on the spear. "Ah, Liban, how long can she force us to serve her evil? What awaits these young mortals, in Caer Wydyr?"

"Sister, all things pass." Liban's voice was lower than Fand's, bleak as the wind. "Remember the Children of Lir, whom the great witch Aife changed into swans. Nine hundred years they were enchanted thus, outcast and fleeing between the land, the sea and the sky; but at last they found rest. So will we, some day. And this mortal, for whom you care so much, knows we are enchanted; she knows we have no choice."

Fand was silent, and Ruth felt wrung with fear. At last Fand nodded. "Yes," she whispered. "Come, sisters."

Ruth climbed into the boat, at the stern. The spears were collected and stacked upright in the prow, inside a metal ring attached to the swan's head. Then the Women pushed the boat down the beach, climbed in and, two to each rowing bench, unshipped the oars. The white blades rose and trembled like wings over the water, dipped, and rose again, scattering drops of emerald. The white boat woke, and glided forward like a bird.

Ruth sat silent on the stern thwart as the Drowned Forest receded and the boat went out over the glittering water, into emptiness. She'd never felt so lost; there was nothing to hold on to in a world so alien. She watched the dark towering of the isle, bulking higher and higher as they approached. The green drift of Undersea thickened in shadowy streams round them and Adam stood in the prow of the boat, his gaze fixed fiercely on the island.

Chapter 6

It was dark on the island, the green mists drifting densely. Like deep water, Ruth thought; the very bottom of the sea. The shapes of the Women, dragging the boat up the beach, were dimmer and more ghostly than ever.

Adam stood by her, staring eagerly through the gloom. Ruth knew he was looking at the glint of Caer Wydyr, which even at this range was difficult to focus on; like something seen in the corner of the eye, it seemed to disappear when you turned to look. Fear fingered Ruth again, and she suppressed a futile burst of anger against Adam.

"How do we get into Caer Wydyr?" he said.

"How should I know?" said Ruth shortly. The great rock looked impossible to climb. But Adam ignored her, glancing round at Fand, who approached now with the other Women. The white faces looked fixed and rigid – locked ever more tightly into their enchantment, Ruth guessed, the closer they came to Fincara.

"Liban and I will lead you," Fand said dully. "Come."

Without looking at either of them, she went ahead. They followed, Adam first, and Fand led them along by the stream. It ran deep and silent, the willows swaying above it; and soon they stood by the foot of the rock. The crags towered over them, smooth and cruel. Halfway up, the stream poured out from some hidden source and fell in a silver smoke down to a pool. Any sound it made was lost in the green murk.

"Now where?" said Adam impatiently.

"Come," said Fand again, stepping up over a spur. She turned, then seemed to disappear behind the waterfall.

Adam sprang up after her, and Ruth set her teeth and followed, slipping on the wet rock. She found herself in a cave, its mouth curtained by the waterfall. There was light, shed faintly from the tip of Fand's spear and reflected in her helmet.

Liban followed, and Fand spoke, her voice eerie in the hollow space. "The way to Caer Wydyr lies in these passages inside the rock. You must follow closely, mortals; watch the light that falls from our spears, and do not turn aside for a moment. Otherwise you will wander these tunnels until you die, for none who lose themselves beneath Caer Wydyr ever find their way out again."

"Come on, then," said Adam, his voice vibrating with eagerness.

Fand looked at him silently – a helpless look, like one powerless to halt destruction. Then she turned and began to climb steps cut in the rock.

Ruth followed Adam. The steps were narrow and winding, and by the time they emerged into a curving tunnel she had lost her sense of direction. She could hear the rush of water, but it seemed to come not from one point but from all around her. She'd expected a steady upward climb, but suddenly the tunnel dipped and steps went down beside a white race of water. The next tunnel forked, turned left, turned right again, and other tunnels led off from it; and Fand led them at an even pace along a course that seemed to have no sense. Ruth's legs were soon aching with climbing steps, only to turn and descend another staircase in the opposite direction.

Gradually she grew so tired she could hardly think. It began to seem impossible that the rock, huge as it was, could contain this labyrinth they were treading. Some of the tunnels must have run for miles, winding in and out of the channels of water that threaded everywhere.

From time to time the passages opened out into caverns, some so gigantic that the glimmer from the two spears was lost in them. One contained a great still lake, and they crossed it along a rock-bridge that sprang dizzily from wall to wall. In another, stalactites reached down to the floor and they walked through a forest of pillars. Here and there water had fretted the walls into tracery, which glittered as the spear-light slid across it; elsewhere, colours had been washed over the rock in a shifting mingle of greens, blues and reds. Ruth's mind seemed to be changing and collapsing with these wonders; and the underground cold ate into her.

At length Fand halted, spear held aloft. Ruth stood dazed and still, conscious only of the chance to rest a moment. The glint from the spear swam in the dark surface of the rock, and, irrelevantly, she noticed her own reflection there – a vague, just-perceptible shape like a shadow. Looking past Adam, she saw Fand had stopped by another set of steps winding up into the rock. She was standing quite still, her raised face lifeless as ivory.

Liban spoke from behind Ruth. "Come, Fand."

Fand didn't move. "Oh Liban!" she whispered. "Can this free us?"

There was a silence, which Adam's voice broke harshly. "Come on!" he cried, pushed past Fand and leapt up the steps two at a time.

Fand stood back, head bowed. Too exhausted really to feel anything, Ruth followed Adam slowly up the steps. It was dark. Fand and Liban came behind, but their spears didn't light the way, only set confusing reflections in the walls. But then a peculiar light began to creep down the steps, mostly blocked by Adam, but searching, sharp, pricking Ruth like needles. Then Adam's shadow vanished; light arrowed down on her; and she was climbing out through a trapdoor into a darkness that dazzled with this stabbing light.

At first she couldn't see. She was slipping on a surface as smooth as glass, and cries were resounding in her ears – her own cries, she thought confusedly, or Adam's; then she fell, and the glassy surface struck like a blow. It was a blow that seemed to stun her whole body; it was hard to get back up again. Coldness sank in like claws, and she looked round, trying to will some life back into her chilled limbs.

She was in the courtyard of Caer Wydyr, the Glass Castle. She could see it clearly now; there were no drifting green currents, just blackness barred by light from the ruins of the Castle. For it was a ruin. The glass battlements were shattered; towers lay in great shards. And from each fragment the light darted, white and spurting, a light that broke the dark but did nothing to dispel it. Ruth had a sense of choking, as if the blackness were too thick to breathe.

She saw Adam painfully getting back to his feet; the floor was glass, cracked everywhere but still smooth and slippery like ice. There was a wild look about him, with the green cloak tossing from his shoulders and light reflected burning in his eyes. "*Fincara!*" he shouted, and the echoes rang back.

A laugh seemed to answer him – almost silent, like a tremor of the light. He swung round, all but falling again; and Ruth saw, standing on a broken parapet above them, a tall figure all in black. Two white hands rose and put back the hood. A long fall of fair hair was shaken free, and green eyes glinted, full of cold laughter.

"I am here, my children," said Fincara.

Ruth no longer had any feeling of being below the sea. This was not Undersea; Caer Wydyr was its own world, a world ruled by enchantment. She looked up at her mother.

Fincara smiled. "Lead them to the Great Tower, Women," she commanded, "where the chains hang."

"No!" Adam shouted and, thrusting Liban aside, plunged towards Fincara – but slipped and crashed down again, helpless. Ruth saw Fincara laugh once more.

"Go, little son, like a good child!" she called, then flung both hands up in a queer quick gesture – and was no longer there.

Adam stared, struggling to get back to his feet; and confusion seemed to burn up in his face. Ruth took a step

67

towards him, but had to stop, afraid of falling. It was Liban who, walking lightly over, took his arm and lifted him.

Ruth felt her own arm gripped, and looked round to see Fand – but the Woman's head was turned away, avoiding her gaze. "Come," Fand whispered dully, and urged her forward. So, leaning on Fand to keep from falling, Ruth crept like a cripple over the glassy floor, between the towers. She looked round once and saw Adam stumbling after her with Liban, his face set in a wild, burning stare.

Chapter 7

The Great Tower was round, a jagged cylinder of glass. Flames seethed along each crack in its wall, and for Ruth, standing on the circular floor, it was like being in the middle of a fire – an icy, silent fire.

All she felt was a kind of blankness; she was now so afraid that she'd become detached, a spectator, not even thinking any more about escape. Before her, the chains Fincara had spoken of hung from a ring in the centre of the roof – three of them, faintly golden when the light blazed. Fand and Liban stood at either side of the door, more stiff and still than ever. And there was Adam. Gradually Ruth looked more and more at him.

If ever a human being burned like a flame, it was Adam. Ruth thought he was hardly aware any more of anything; his eyes seemed blind, and his hands were clenched, but whether from pain or exaltation Ruth couldn't say. Then suddenly he bowed his head between his fists and cried out: "Fincara! *Mother!*"

Ruth shut her eyes, flinching. When she opened them again, Fincara was there, as silently as if the blackness had merely thickened into shape. Laughter flickered round her lips, and the green eyes seemed to cast their glances everywhere.

"What a shout," she said drily. "What's ado, my son, that you call so loud?"

Gasping, Adam stared at her. Ruth wanted to reach out and pull him back, as if he were moving towards a precipice. His eyes, burning, were full of confusion.

He took a step towards Fincara, but the floor inside the Tower was the same slippery glass, and he fell to one knee. "I've come to find you!" he cried, struggling back to his feet; but the words seemed to blur into a shout that was almost meaningless.

"Indeed!" Fincara's voice quivered, alive with mockery. She flung out her hands. "Well, come then – you're old enough to walk unaided now!"

Adam lunged towards her, but lost his footing and crashed down again. Fincara's maddening laughter rippled out, and she stepped over to him as easily as a dancer. Ruth saw her feet were bare.

"Come to find me?" she repeated, reaching down to grip his arm and heaving him to his feet. "When I had to send the Women to fetch you every step of the way, child – and pick you up every time you fell? Why, you were not very clever in your search!"

Adam straightened, and suddenly Fincara seemed small, for he was as tall as her, looking levelly into her eyes; but while hers still laughed, his were savage with bewilderment.

"I could have found you," he said, gasping, "whatever you did!"

"Could you so?" said Fincara, as if to a very small boy. "And what would you have done then?"

Adam stared, brow knitting painfully. He opened his mouth, then shut it again.

"Why," said Fincara mockingly, "you must have had something in mind!" She seized his wrists, not gently, and clapped his hands on to her shoulders. "There – you've found me! Now what, son of mine?"

Adam gripped her shoulders, and his gaze burnt, yet seemed to wander helplessly. Ruth's spine began to creep; any moment Fincara would start to laugh again.

At last Adam spoke, as if each word was a weight he had to lift. "Take – you – and – find – Jake – too . . ."

"Indeed!" Fincara cried, and struck Adam's hands from her shoulders. "So I was to be delivered back to that fool, was I? Why, you're as big a fool, my son – but go on, let's hear to the end. Find me, find Jake – then what?"

Adam stared at Fincara, but his face seemed like an old garment that wouldn't fit any more. Ruth could hardly bear to watch.

"He doesn't know!" Fincara cried, laughter shrilling. "I thought at least to hear we were to live happy ever after! Oh, little son, what a pig's ear you've made!"

Adam turned, and without a sound fell to one knee, casting an arm over his face. The green cloak sank in folds round him, and he was as still as a statue. For Ruth it was almost as if he died before her eyes.

Fincara's white hand came down and stroked his hair. Silence seemed to grow and thicken, then, in the burning tower. "There now, my honey," Fincara murmured. "There now, my little love; there now. What's all this fuss for, all this trouble and struggling? You had but to wait till your mother called you; sit on your chair and suck your thumb, keeping quiet until I come . . . There's only one thing you were born to do, my child; only one thing to trouble your head about . . ."

Ruth stared, hardly believing. Hadn't she humiliated him enough, without taunting him with baby-talk? Suddenly a wave of fear washed over her mind and she became tinglingly aware, as if she hadn't realized it before, what danger they were in. A pulse of light slid over Fincara's face, and the long green eyes were so alight, so blazingly concentrated, that she seemed a different woman.

"Listen," Fincara whispered. "Let me explain your birth to you, my child. Your mother was a witch's daughter, born in your world but not in your time – long before that, in a time when they feared witches and hung them from the gallows tree. Listen! It won't be a long story . . . Came a day when your mother walked along the strand at Starr Hills and knew that tomorrow, or the next day, or the day after that, the stupid peasants would come and take away your grannie to the witch-finder, prick her for witch-marks, watch her till she maddened from sleeplessness, then swim her in the river. And your mother knew she herself would be the next one; for when the mob have killed one witch, they always go searching for another. And your mother thought to herself, honey, of the short life ahead of her, of all the worth and power within her and the little use it would be, and she felt such

72

a weeping bitterness that she cursed humankind. Ah! When I remember . . . "

Ruth stared through the flashing darkness, and despite the cold felt her blood pulsing. Starr Hills. Everything always seemed to lead back to that place. Briefly she saw in her mind a slender girl walking the shore, beating her hands one against the other in bitter rebellion. And she felt the picture had always been there, waiting only to wake.

"Listen," Fincara said quietly. "Do you know what happened then, my son?"

Adam lowered his arm and looked up – a strange blind look, full of fire. "Yes," he said thickly, and Ruth's heart beat hard. What was Fincara doing to him? How *could* he know?

"Tell, then, little one. Come! Say it . . . "

Words came from Adam in a toneless chant: "Then the sea rose in a great wave and swept away the witch's daughter, and she was never seen on Starr Hills again . . . "

Ruth almost choked. The old story: Gran had told it to them years ago. She stared at Fincara unbelievingly.

"So it did!" Fincara cried, and light flared over them – the woman's laughing face, and Adam's burning blindness. "For I called on the sea to bear me away, and I came down to this isle and took it for my own. And here I dwelt, perfecting my powers, far away from stupid humankind . . . and now I am more powerful than any. For I found the Dagda's Cauldron – Undry."

Ruth looked to Adam to see if that word, Undry, would rouse him. He didn't stir.

"Regard Caer Wydyr, my son," Fincara said softly. "Long ago Manannan and the Dagda raised it, a shining Glass Castle in the west of the world, guarding against the dark. And in the Great Tower, from three golden chains in the roof, the Dagda hung a Cauldron named Undry – a wondrous thing, with pearls at its rim, full of water and changing light. To drink the waters of Undry would heal any hurt, still any grief, and bring understanding of every mystery that weighs on human-kind. So it was called the Cauldron of Wisdom."

Ruth was beginning to feel chillingly alone, as Fincara whispered into Adam's ears and he knelt there motion-less. Was Fincara just telling a story – or was it an enchantment, her way of casting a spell? Phrase by phrase, syllable by syllable, a bewitchment seemed to be building up round Adam; Ruth almost thought he shone with his own light now, like a flame. And Fincara's voice was going on, clear and murmurous. Despite herself, she listened . . .

"But when the mortal race grew so great, child, wonders were no more seen in the world; Undry was lost, and even the Glass Castle was gone from the west. It was I who raised it again, with my magic art – summoning it back to sight here on my island. Yet even I cannot raise these ruins higher or make whole these broken walls –not until Undry is restored in its old power! For I found Undry . . ." The fire leapt in a glimmering sheet – and sank, leaving a deeper, dazzled dark.

Ruth searched through it desperately for Adam. Pres-ently she could see him again; his head was erect, but his eyes were cast down so that she could only see the dark.

curve of eyelashes. Yet still he seemed to blaze. Fincara's white hand lay on his forehead, commanding him.

"I found Undry," Fincara whispered, slow and measured. "In Andernesse I saw it, and sent my Women to fetch it for me. Poor Undry! All the magic had died from it, and it was but a husk of itself; for all my art, it could tell me only one thing – that no one could restore it to its place except a child not yet born, and born only for that task. After much thought, my son, I knew there was one simple way to make such a child."

The white fire blazed, sank and blazed again. And a hand seemed to grip Ruth's heart; for she understood, suddenly, everything Fincara had done.

"I took Undry, little one," Fincara whispered. "Poor Undry, shrunken and wasted! – and I left the sea and went up on to the land, into the world of mortals. I had it in my mind to seek a time and place where I should meet with a man called mad by his fellows, for if such a man spoke strange things of me, none would heed him. And my magic wrought true – for it was into your time I came, to Starr Hills, where I had walked four hundred years before; and coming to meet me was a man who asked me simply if I were a mermaid, for he had seen me walking out of the sea."

It was strange, in that raging cold, to feel the hotness of tears. Jake, Ruth thought to herself, *oh, Jake . . .*

"I gave him water to drink, my child, from Undry. Some memory of magic still clung to it, and with my art there was enough; he drank, looked into my eyes, and could never again think of any other woman. In time, I bore his child; and so you came crying into the world, my

75

son, protesting against life . . . " She looked at Adam, the green eyes glittering. *"Now do you see, child?"*

Adam knelt motionless, globed in fire. Then all at once he looked up, with a stare so sudden and urgent it was like a shout. Ruth almost heard his voice – "Fincara! *Mother!"*

"No, no, my little one!" Fincara cried, and her laughter overflowed. She put both hands on Adam's head. "Why, how strong and wilful you've grown! Come, I'll spell it out for you – one thing only you were born for, and that's to live fourteen years and then bring Undry here and hang it from these chains. No more! There's only one reason for you, Adam Demdyke! Only one – no other!"

Adam stared up at her. Ruth saw he couldn't move; the only life left to him was in his eyes, burning. And then the very fire seemed to swallow him up, blurring him from Ruth's sight. Fincara laughed again, shook back her hair and began to sing.

If the song began with human words, they soon melted into words no human voice could ever form – words like the sea rushing, whirlpools thrumming. Ruth found herself crouching on the floor, almost fainting; wondering how she could ever have thought before that Fincara was casting spells. For a time it overcame her, and she seemed to drift in black depths.

When at last she looked up, it seemed days, weeks later. She saw Adam kneeling erect and motionless, his face turned up to the chains; his eyes were closed, and fire burned clear and transparent all round him. In his white face, there was nothing but a stillness deeper than the farthest depths of the sea – a quietness that made Ruth think of a drowned body drifting on its slow journey down to the sea bed. And Fincara stood by, her hands folded in front of her, looking thoughtfully down at her son. She seemed, Ruth thought, satisfied.

Chapter 8

Ruth wasn't conscious of moving, but perhaps she shivered – or perhaps the light touched her, reminding Fincara she was there. All at once the long green eyes were glittering at her.

"So," said Fincara; "the little daughter, too."

If the cold had not completely numbed Ruth by now, she would have shuddered. Fincara seemed so tall, surrounded by the white fire; before her, Ruth felt helpless.

"What – what have you done to Adam?" she whispered, and her voice came whimpering, like a frightened child's.

Fincara laughed. "Made him himself again, little girl, that's all. Have you not listened? He was born to bring Undry here to me, and now he knows it. I've called back into his mind the spells I put on him at his birth. He shall stay under the chains for a night and a day, and when he wakes he shall remember nothing else."

Ruth looked at Adam and could hardly recognize him. He was so white, so still, she couldn't believe it was really him.

It was a bad moment as she crouched there, looking at him. He was bewitched, she could see that; changed into something else, as Fand and the other Women had been – something that had nothing to do with his real self. And there was no reason to think the same wouldn't happen to her now . . . but must she really be overcome like that, so helplessly? A flicker of rebellion stole into her mind and, as if it had needed that impetus, one clear thought struggled free. "Why do you talk as if you and Jake had only one child?" she whispered. "I was born too – *before* Adam!"

Fincara threw back her head and laughed, a clear pitch of mirth. "Oh, my daughter! So you were – but as soon as they put you in my arms I could see you were no use to me!"

"What do you mean?"

"Child, you'll never – never know!" Again Fincara's laughter streamed out; it was difficult to bear, and Ruth tried to turn her head away; but in a moment the laughter had melted into song, clear and cold like raindrops tracking a windowpane. Frozen as she was, Ruth felt a shudder going down her spine. She had to look up at the glittering green eyes; she couldn't help herself; she had to watch as Fincara stooped down before her, white hands on knees, and sang –

> *From thy mother, in Undersea,*
> *Witch's power comes to thee.*
> *But you'll never know, my child,*
> *Never know, my silly daughter,*
> *How to work the magic wild*

Of Undersea, of underwater.
This my spell on you is laid:
You'll be always too afraid.

She could feel the enchantment in the words, the song from thirteen years back doubling with the fierce bewitchment of the moment – her eyes were dulling, the smell of the sea overcoming her, her mind sinking away as if into deep water. It came to her that being bewitched was like drowning, dark and easy.

She didn't understand what happened next. At first she thought it was a burst of panic, which didn't surprise her, knowing what a coward she was. But it grew and grew, like a great impossible wave gathering, till she knew it must be something from outside herself; she heard her voice crying words of some kind, as if impelled. Then the wave broke.

It seemed to kill her. It wasn't like Fincara's magic; this was the whole ocean in storm and thunder. No one could survive it. Dimly she saw the Great Tower peak in a cone of white flame; Adam seemed not to move, but Fand and Liban fell, and Fincara staggered before the sheeting fire. Then raging darkness overwhelmed her and she was being smashed, pounded to pieces, and it would be better when she died properly and couldn't feel it any more.

Gradually it passed; the great wave ebbed, and she became aware of Fand and Liban climbing shakily back to their feet, and Fincara screaming something at them. Her head was ringing like an empty glass. She wasn't surprised when she raised her hand and could see nothing before her eyes. That was how she felt – snuffed out, like a candle.

"Find her!" It was a spitting shout; Fincara flung out her hands, and the white fire came leaping again. "The little hag! She's called up her magic and made herself invisible! But I'll have no such tricks played on my island!"

That roused Ruth a little. She stared at the glass of the Tower, where reflections appeared by moments – Fand, Liban, Adam, Fincara. But not herself. It was true. She'd become invisible. But . . . *magic*? *Her* magic?

"Find her!" Fincara screeched. "Use your spears, fools – see what blood they'll draw from the air!"

Ruth flinched. But she couldn't seem to gather her wits; all she wanted to do was kneel there weeping. What's *happened* to me, her mind kept repeating, stupidly; what's *happened*?

Liban turned in her direction with a levelled spear, and it was only then that she understood she must escape. That was easy; no longer slipping on the glass, she glided out through the empty doorway, into the burning ruins. It didn't feel as if she had a body at all.

She didn't go far; there seemed no point. Coming to a stop, she struggled to understand what had happened to her. Magic had descended from somewhere and made her invisible; and in the process it had . . . well, it felt as if it had killed her. Ruth Demdyke was simply not there any more. Surely this was how it felt to be dead – empty all through, and cold. Frozen cold. True, she'd escaped Fincara, but Fincara would only have bewitched her, not killed her.

Everything's changed, she thought, and the word tolled in her mind – changed, changed, changed. Till now she'd been able to cope, after a fashion; even going dumb with terror had been a way of coping. But not now. Nothing could be the same after this. It was like stepping from a lit room into illimitable, unknowable night.

If I'd known, she thought – and stopped short. Then, forcing herself, she put the thought into words: If I'd known, I wouldn't have used magic.

But she *hadn't*! How could she? The magic had just come, trampling her in its path; she wasn't a witch, like Fincara!

The thought wouldn't go away.

This is no good, she told herself, as the fierce ruins burnt round her. Even if I'm dead, there's no point just standing here; and if I'm not, I've got to escape.

At once she was conscious of hopeless difficulties. How could she find her way through the labyrinth in the rock? How was she to cross the river? How could she get back to her own world? How, above all, was she to become visible again?

It was no good thinking about any of these things. If she really was dead none of them mattered anyway. Wearily she forced herself to move through the Castle, and presently found the trapdoor. She climbed down into the dark. It felt kind, after the bitter dazzle of the ruins.

And in the pitch black, it seemed she had some sort of body after all; distantly she could sense hands feeling their way, feet stumbling. It was all quite useless, of course; she'd no idea where she was going. The darkness was suffocatingly thick, and she knew that ordinarily she'd have been terrified.

Time passed. Then she saw, far away, glimmers of light

crossing the passage ahead of her. At first she thought it was her eyes playing tricks (did she have eyes?), but then she recognized it: the glow cast by the Women's spears. So they'd been sent down into the rock, no doubt still with orders to draw blood from the air.

She stood, watching. If Fincara was trying to kill her, did that mean she wasn't dead? Presently the lights passed and she was in the dark again; and she went on, feeling her way. She still knew it was hopeless. And that was proved when, quite soon, her foot collided softly with rock. She felt with her hands. She'd come to a dead end.

She looked back over her shoulder and saw the light of a spear approaching. It came towards her steadily. She saw the glint of a silver helmet and the slender figure of a Woman. The spear-tip, glinting, pointed straight at her.

She turned to face it, her back against the rock. The passage was too narrow to let her slip past the Woman. This would finally prove whether she was dead or not. She watched the bright spark of the spear approaching, and felt nothing but a dull kind of relief.

It paused, perhaps three feet from her. The Woman's head was bent slightly, so that the helm shadowed her face. And then her whisper came, softly: "Mortal – it is I, Fand. If you are present, appear to me!"

Ruth's heart gave a heave, and suddenly all the frozen emptiness seemed to go melting through her, changed to burning tears. Her eyes blurred; she blinked to clear them, and saw a faint reflection of herself swimming in the rock, cast there by the spear-light. And Fand's eyes

83

met hers, all their depths waking in recognition.

"Oh, Fand —" Ruth said, and stopped, her voice shaking. She felt dizzy and slid awkwardly to the ground, leaning her head on her hand.

Fand set her spear against the wall and knelt by Ruth, reaching out to touch her hand. "Mortal . . . " There was a new note in her voice, stirring like music. "It is as I thought. You are stronger than your mother; she cannot vanquish you!"

Stronger? She'd never felt so weak, so helpless. "I don't know what you mean," Ruth said huskily.

"Let me tell you." Fand looked different to Ruth; there was life in her face, as if Fincara's spells had lost some of their hold. "She married with your father, seeking to have a child who would restore Undry to the Glass Castle; but when you were born, she saw you had all her magic, and more. She dared not use you to bring back Undry. So she waited till your brother was born, and laid all her spells on him."

Ruth shivered. "She laid a spell on me too . . . "

"Yes – to forget your magic, never to use it! She is afraid of you. She is afraid you are waking from her spell, casting it off. She bade us bring you here, so that she could sing it over you again."

Ruth felt numb. "But *I* can't work magic."

"Mortal – how else did you vanish from our sight in the Great Tower?"

"No!" The word came from Ruth with such force it startled her. "I haven't any magic! I don't know how I turned invisible – it must have been Fincara's spell going wrong. It wasn't me!"

Fand was silent a moment, gazing at Ruth; then she

84

bent her head. "No," she said, low. "I know Fincara's magic; it was none of hers. Mortal, I have never felt such great power wielded. Truly, all the oceans would rise if you commanded them!"

Ruth pressed her lips together, guarding against a second outburst. *From thy mother, in Undersea, witch's power comes to thee* ... She knew now it was something she couldn't face, to be possessed of magic – magic that could explode without warning and all but kill you ... "No," she said unsteadily. "I *can't*, Fand!"

Fand sighed, so faintly that Ruth hardly heard. "Poor mortal," she whispered.

Ruth was silent, trying to pull herself together. She still felt queer and different, her old self refusing to come back. Changed, she thought, changed ... I must get home, back to the things I know; maybe I'll start to feel right again then. "Fand – how do I get back to my own world?"

"It will be difficult, without magic," said Fand sombrely. She thought, and then spoke again, low. "Night comes here, as to other lands. We must hide until it is dark, and then I will steal a coracle and row you to the Drowned Forest. The trees remember the upper world; there are ways there to return. Do not fear, mortal ... " she raised her head, gazing full and steady " ... I will come with you, and protect you with my spear from whatever befalls."

Ruth caught her breath. "But Fand – what about Fincara's spell? If you help me, won't you ... ?" It was hard to say. "Won't you die?"

Fand smiled. It was only a faint smile, glimmering, but more than Ruth had ever thought she'd see from Fand.

"If I summon all my strength, for a short time I can act against her spells," she whispered. "Ah, mortal, when first I called you to the pool in the Forest, you came swift as a bird – and I felt then that our souls answered to each other. I do not know why. Perhaps only because we are both bound by her spells. But her magic cannot hold you; you are beginning to be free. I would give all my life for that to happen."

"But Fand —"

"No," Fand whispered, looking up at her. "Better to die for this, than live to help the dark powers conquer. Come, mortal. Let us find a place to hide until nightfall."

Ruth rose, her heart beating with a confusion of emotions – but predominant was a sense of *rightness*, that she and Fand should unite against Fincara. Never in her life had she felt so sure of anyone, as she did then of this enchanted warrior woman. Yet she hesitated. "Fand," she said, low. "First I've got to go back into the Castle and get my brother."

There was a moment's silence; then Fand clasped her hands to her face, as if seized by more dismay than she could bear. "Mortal – do not, do not!" she whispered. "He is lost to you; he is utterly bewitched! Never have I seen Fincara's magic so possess anyone's spirit – flee from him, mortal! He will bring the Women straight to us!"

Ruth stood still – wondering, with only a kind of weariness, at what point she'd determined to return into that burning castle for Adam. And why? She was such a stranger to herself now; it was no use trying to understand anything she did. She said, "He's the one who has to

86

bring Undry back, Fand. I can't get it for you, without him."

Fand raised her face, slowly. "Ah, mortal – I have grown older, this past day. I am too wise now to believe I can buy my freedom with Undry; Fincara will never release us. But you can be free!"

Ruth had to look away, ashamed; what had she ever done for Fand, except break that promise to her? "I will bring you Undry; I promise, Fand. But Adam . . ." She gave up trying to justify herself. "He's my brother. Please, Fand – will you help me?"

There was a silence, while Fand looked at her – a silence deep with foreboding. Then Fand reached out and took her spear. "Follow close, mortal. And tread without sound, lest the Women hear. It will be dangerous, going back into the Castle."

Chapter 9

Back inside the Great Tower, Ruth ached with the cold. Now she was visible again, she'd had to take off her shoes in order to walk on the glass floor without slipping, and she couldn't feel her feet. The Castle burnt, spitting through the dark.

Fand, standing guard outside the Tower, had warned her to hurry. The Castle was deserted now, but there was no telling when Fincara and the Women would return. Fincara, surely, would have some magic way of tracking them down.

But Ruth was hesitating. It was difficult to approach Adam. He knelt inside a globe of pale fire, his face lifted to the chains, his eyes closed. He seemed far away from Ruth, in a trance whose nature she could only guess at – but free, she thought, of the despair and anger that beset him in their own world. His face was full of stillness. She thought: I ought to leave him here.

She pushed the thought away, afraid even to think it; Adam had to be rescued and that was that. She seized his shoulders and shook him, hard. "Adam! *Adam!*"

He gave no sign of hearing, but a faint shrill cry seemed to echo distantly. It's inside my head, Ruth thought; I'm such a coward, I hear things that aren't there. She set her lips and dragged Adam out of the fire, hooking one of his arms round her neck. He leaned on her, not wholly unconscious, but she could tell he didn't know what was happening to him. "Adam!" she whispered, but he still seemed not to hear.

Abruptly, the pale fire sank and vanished, leaving only the glare from the ruins. And another cry rang in her ears, or inside her head; she was feeling dizzy with the cold, and couldn't tell which. Half carrying and half dragging Adam, she got him outside. "Fand . . . "

"Hush!" She felt Fand grip her arm; the white face turned, whiter than before as a gust of fire passed. "The Women have come," Fand whispered, lips close to her ear. "They are searching the Castle; and they have set a guard on the trapdoor."

Behind a splintered wall, Ruth saw the spark of a spear move. Hurriedly she took a fresh grip on Adam and pulled him round the side of a broken column, out of sight. "What do we do now, then?" she whispered.

"We must try to hide." Fand looked stranger than ever, her face fixed and old as if she were withering in this icy fire. "Our only escape would be to climb down the face of the rock; but . . . " her eyes rested on Adam " . . . your brother could not do it, mortal. We must find a place in the ruins to hide until we can rouse him. I know such a place. Come . . . "

Ruth followed her, dragging Adam. The place was a collapsed wall, where it was possible to edge between two glittering spars of glass into a kind of cave underneath the rubble. Ruth went first with Adam, manhandling him

89

in; the roof was a cracked slab wedged at an angle, and there was only room to stand. Even inside, the shards flashed and spat with white fire, and seemed to radiate cold. "It's horrible in here, Fand!" Ruth gasped.

"It is the only hiding place there is, mortal." Fand stood inside the opening with her spear. Her whisper, all but drowned in the hiss of the flames, sounded fluttery and frail. "Hush; be still; be silent; and the Women may pass us by . . ."

Ruth noticed, with a tightening of the throat, that she could see through the glass rubble. Not easily – shapes were misty and distorted, blotted out completely when the fire flared; but if she could see out, presumably the Women could see in. The only chance was to stay perfectly still, and hope the flashing fire would mask them from sight.

Then Adam stirred, lifting his head, and she looked down straight into his eyes. They were half open, silently fixing her in a look so intense and piercing that she felt caught in it, as if hypnotized. Somehow she knew he was still in his trance, but urgently calling her, urgently trying to communicate . . . she stared, fighting to understand. But then his eyes closed again, his head sinking to one side.

She looked up at Fand. It was difficult to see her through the dazzling spurts of fire; she seemed to be less and less there. Ruth was only certain of her eyes, where the reflected flames flashed tinily.

"Mortal . . ." Her whisper was fainter than ever. "Can you not raise your magic? Else all will be lost; the Women will find us; your brother in his enchantment will call them."

Surely Adam was in no state to call anyone. "I told you," Ruth said hoarsely, turning her head away, "I can't make magic."

Fand said no more. Looking through the rubble, Ruth saw the whole Castle was alive with the sparks of spears. She could see the Women now too, their cloaks whipping out in the gusts of fire. There seemed to be so many of them, more and more crowding silently through the ruins wherever she looked. It's only magic, she thought, remembering Fand's words; but that was hard to believe, and no comfort anyway, knowing as she did now what magic could do. Fire kept flashing in the cave, dazzling her, and it was getting harder and harder to think clearly. Ruth only knew that all her hope was pinned on Fand to get her and Adam out of this. I don't care about anything but being safe, she thought; I believed I cared about Fand, but I don't, I'm too much of a coward – I just want her to save me, and then I don't care what happens to her. Of all crazinesses, to come back into this Castle . . . She felt as if she were sinking deeper and deeper in her own panic, her whole consciousness going down into a quicksand while her body stood there, stupid with fear.

Then it happened. She felt Adam's ribs swell suddenly as he took in a huge breath; he thrust her away from him, siezed hold of the roof slab as if to pull it down on top of them; and screamed. It was a great wordless whoop that echoed round the Castle, and Ruth saw all the spears swerve towards them. Adam hauled at the roof and the whole cave lurched, falling.

Ruth was conscious of Fand seizing her wrist; then she and Adam were both sprawling outside, Fand on her knees beside them, while the rubble slid crashing in a

91

cloud of brilliant dust, obliterating the cave. Her first thought was to stop Adam screaming again, and she lunged for him, trying to get her hand over his mouth; but he was too strong for her. All she could do was twine her arms round him and try to anchor him by her weight against the still-shuddering rubble, so that at least their backs were protected. There was a shrieking in her ears, so vibratingly shrill that for an instant she thought it was the whole Glass Castle shivering to pieces – then she looked up and saw the Women sweeping down on them, screaming their war cry.

There were thousands of them. They seemed part of the Castle's fire, each flame a plunging spear; and Ruth was beyond remembering this was only magic. Briefly she looked for Liban, but the faces were all the same – white as fire, empty as death.

Numbly she saw Fand step in front of her and Adam, spear raised. The Women never paused, but thrust at her, spears hissing. Only Fand was attacked; Ruth guessed she and Adam were to be taken alive. And Fand didn't try to counter-attack, only parrying again and again with the shaft of her spear, gripped in her two hands. Ruth saw she couldn't last long; her face had a blind look, as if she could no longer see through the dazzling fire.

Ruth knew she had to do something. Adam seemed to have sunk back into his trance, and she got to her feet, leaving him lying. She gripped two icy lumps of rubble, meaning to throw them – but the host was so great; it would be useless. She looked at Fand, seeing the white arms shake, and knowing that in another moment a spear would go home and Fand would die; because of me, she thought, all because of me. *Help us*, she implored silently, not knowing whom she spoke to, and for a moment her despair went on mounting. But then an answer came.

It was like the blood pounding in her temples; a mutter, a surge, like a great wave gathering far away. Ruth looked up sharply, and then realized, sickeningly, what it was she had called.

She dropped the shards and pushed forward past Fand, bare hands stretched out against the spears; she couldn't help herself. The Women's fierce shrilling cry paused; thinned; they edged back, spear-points sinking in sudden silence. "Go!" Ruth shouted hoarsely. "Get away from here! Get back into the rock – you mustn't stay here!"

There was a mutter of indrawn breath; lost eyes regarding her. She saw Fand drop her spear and sink to the ground as light as a feather, eyes closed and pale hair streaming. Then the surge in her head became a roar, blotting out everything. Desperately she turned back to Adam, somehow seizing his arm; she was conscious of his silent eyes again, dark slits urgently calling to her. Then she knew nothing but the breaking wave, the sound of her voice crying out long strange words, and the power crushing her. Great lights seemed to go past her, shaped like warriors. Ruth heard her words die away into silence, and knew the Women had been conquered. She still had hold of Adam, and gripped a little tighter; then closed her eyes. She knew this time that she was probably still alive, but it didn't feel like it.

*

93

"Mortal." The voice was clear and faintly ringing, like crystal – yet deep, a man's voice. "Rouse yourself."

Ruth stayed still, eyes closed. Gradually she became aware of waves falling on a shore close by, and the air was sweet to breathe, with a tingle like clearest light. With an effort she looked up.

She was kneeling on a beach of golden sand. Before her a green sea rippled, melting into azure where it met the sky. Adam lay slumped and motionless beside her. The air was so full of sunlight that Ruth, drained and weary, winced from it. She let go of Adam's arm and rose; then looked up at the man who stood there.

She wasn't sure if he was a man. He was taller than any human being she had ever seen, and his hair, a pale gold streaked with silver, seemed to be lifted from his brow in a wind she couldn't feel. His eyes were as golden as a hawk's, but so still and intent they awed her faintly. His clothes were not splendid – a scuffed, scratched leather jerkin, a shirt of coarse linen, and trousers of faded woollen cloth. And his face was lined, though at first she'd thought him young.

It was hard to meet his eyes for long, and she looked away. The beach shelved up to green slopes, and quite near she could see a forest begin. Oaks, birches and pines stood whispering to themselves; she saw sunshine slanting into a succession of glades, on to turf starred with mallow and ragged robin, and the gold of last year's leaves. Streams wound down to the shore, murmuring.

Ruth let her eyes dwell on the forest. It seemed to her that the only thing worth doing was to walk deep into those glades, far away from everything; she thought of lingering by the streams and watching the sunlight move, in silence.

She looked back at the man and said, "Where is this?"

His brows drew together. "This is the Forest of Andernesse. Did you not know?"

"No," said Ruth. "What's Andernesse?"

He was silent a moment, as if something troubled him. Then he said quietly, "Andernesse is the Last Land of Otherworld. Once all the countries of Otherworld were ruled by the powers of light; but for years now darkness has been growing. For a time we fought against the gathering shadows, but to little avail. The City of Findias fell in the south, and Gorias in the east, and then Falias in the north; and at last Murias, the Crystal Isle, sank into the western sea and was lost. Then we, the half-mortals, withdrew to Andernesse and built a great spell-wall around us, to prevent the powers of the dark from entering. And so we have lived for many an age."

Ruth looked at him emptily. The words, especially the names – Findias, Falias, Murias – seemed to shimmer in her mind like strong light, and she knew it was important to understand what was being said to her; but still she felt leaden. Half-mortals . . . Jake had spoken of them to Adam, in a sentence too mad to understand. She said, with an effort, "What are half-mortals?"

He studied her, faintly frowning. "Once there was a race of immortals in Otherworld," he said gravely. "They wedded with humans, and we are their sons. Only a few of us remain, for though we do not age as mortals do, we can be killed, or in great unhappiness can choose to die."

Ruth was silent. Fand had spoken of marrying an immortal; Manannan, she remembered.

"Mortal," said the man, his voice deepening, "did you truly not know these things?"

"No," said Ruth. "How could I?"

He gazed at her, searchingly. "One called upon the half-mortals, using words of such power that we were compelled to come instantly, breaking the spell-wall and leaving Andernesse undefended for the first time since the Four Cities fell. Who called, mortal?"

It was hard to answer. But it was quite clear this time what the answer must be; she'd felt herself call the magic, felt it respond to her. *From thy mother, in Undersea, witch's power comes to thee* . . . Nor did she think she could hide anything from this man with the golden eyes.

"It was me," she said.

"You?" The man stared, and urgency entered his voice. "Who taught you this magic? Where did you learn the words which summon us?"

"I don't know," Ruth said dully. "What words were they? I can't remember."

He frowned; then his face softened faintly. "Come," he said, "tell me your name, mortal, and the name of this lad who lies like one dead."

"He isn't dead," Ruth said bleakly. "He's bewitched. There's a spell on him to bring Undry back to Undersea."

"There are mysteries here," said the man. "Who knows where Undry is, in these days?"

"We do," said Ruth.

"You?" He stared again; then his voice strengthened, light seeming to spread from him. "Mortal, if you hold Undry, return it to us! Long ago it was stolen from us, and we hold the memory of it dear; now that the powers of darkness have grown so strong, Andernesse is the one safe place for it. Undry must be returned!"

Everyone says that to me, Ruth thought; everyone wants me to bring them Undry . . . and I've promised it to Fand, but I don't know now whether she's alive or dead. "Please—" she said.

He was silent, watching her.

"Please," said Ruth, "it was you who rescued us from Caer Wydyr, wasn't it? What happened to the Women? Did you – kill them?"

He shook his head. Lines deepened on his face, making him look gaunt and worn. "It was an evil place you called us to, mortal. Many an age has passed since I last descended to Undersea; I did not know the dark powers had such a grip on it. But the Women fled from us. They seemed in fear. Though in truth they had little need; the last time we fought, they vanquished us easily . . . " He was silent a moment, his face bleak. "We harmed none of them. We only brought you and the boy as swiftly as we could to Andernesse."

Ruth was silent. It was the best answer she could have expected; but the memory of Fand sinking to the ground preyed on her.

"Mortal," the man said after a moment, "tell me this: where did you learn your magic?"

Ruth looked away. "I didn't," she said unevenly. "It just happens. I don't know why. I never asked to be a witch's daughter."

97

"So," he said quietly, and looked out to sea as if he understood she couldn't bear his gaze just then. "It is hard to read another's heart. I have known those to whom the gift of enchantment was sheer delight; who sparkled with their powers like fireflies after nightfall. Yet also have I known souls near break with the weight and strangeness of it. Mortal, I cannot help you."

Ruth already knew that; no one could help. Yet it was some relief just to speak. "It makes me feel so alone," she said. "As if I'm just a ghost come back to haunt – not real at all."

He turned to look straight at her. "Those who call upon great powers are consumed like tinder – emptied out like water. This is no childish game, mortal. You called the half-mortals out of Andernesse, and broke the spell-wall which was the last and greatest protection against the dark. I cannot tell what will come from this day's work."

Ruth stood silent; these urgent words only made the deadness inside her worse. Presently he reached out a hand and touched her forehead, and Ruth felt something enter her – not comfort, not relief, but a sense of light: clear shining spaces which pain could inhabit but not overwhelm. She tightened her lips, mastering herself.

"There," said the man, rather sadly. "Even Diancecht's son can do no more to ease a troubled heart. Mortal, my name is Miach, and I am accounted a healer. Come; let us see if aught can be done for the boy here."

He knelt down by Adam, turning him over on to his

back. Adam's eyes were closed, in some state that looked colder and more complicated than sleep.

"Take your cloak off, mortal," Miach said, unfastening Adam's. "It is not good to wear the garments of the Sea People over-long."

Ruth took off the cloak, shivering – though, if anything, the sun seemed to reach her more warmly now. She rolled the two cloaks into a bundle and laid them down on the shore where the tide could come and take them. Miach, his hand on Adam's brow and his head bowed, seemed to listen. Ruth saw that the light in this place didn't come only from the sun; a faint glow fell from Miach, something like starlight – cool and pure, with colours at its heart.

Miach withdrew his hand and looked up at her, a shadow over his face. "Mortal," he said, "there is a cloud like death round this lad. So strong is the spell on him, I know none who could undo it; it draws on his own nature, and all his strength serves but to bind it tighter. One might think his own mother had bewitched him, before ever he left her belly."

Ruth's heart sank. Had it all been useless, then? "Will he wake up?" she said. "Will he remember who he is?"

"Perhaps." Miach touched Adam's forehead again, broodingly. "Few enchantments can sink the human soul entirely; some memory, some will, remains. But this is sea magic, deep and drowning . . . I do not know, mortal."

"But he's my brother," said Ruth bleakly. "What can I do?"

99

The answer came from behind her, in stern tones that shook the golden air. "Leave here, and take him with you; for Andernesse is not to be trodden by mortals, and already you have harmed us enough!"

Ruth jerked round, the sheer force of that voice turning her. At once she was dazzled.

They were beings like Miach, a crowd of them walking down to the shore from the forest. Some were even taller than Miach, and some were dark-haired and pale-skinned, with eyes more silver than gold. A few wore breastplates and helmets, but the metal was dull and dinted, and their clothes too were stained and poor. Yet they all seemed to stand in that wind Ruth couldn't feel, and she knew she was in the presence of men greater than kings. Light flowed from them, full of faint colours that sparked and changed and faded, difficult to see in the sunshine. Ruth wanted to hide her face in her hands.

"Ilbrec," said Miach, rising. His voice seemed deeper and fuller now that he spoke to his own kind; echoes moved in the light. "She says they hold Undry. In truth, there seems something more than common about them."

"I have no heart to listen to the talk of humans!" It was the stern voice again, greater than Miach's and full of anger. The tallest of the men looked down at Ruth; his hair was bright silver, and his gold eyes were like an eagle's. "I know naught of how you came into this plight, girl, and I care little enough, but this I know – you have broken the spell-wall and opened Andernesse to the powers of the dark! The one safe stronghold left in Other-world and you must needs breach it!"

Ruth looked down, utterly unable to meet his eyes. Yet it was unjust, this anger; she hadn't known her magic would call the half-mortals – she'd never meant it to. She hadn't even heard of them, until this moment...

Miach said urgently, "Ilbrec, we should question her. In this place she called us to, Caer Wydyr, a great evil is growing."

"No greater than the breaching of Andernesse!" Ilbrec's anger was like vast waves of light rolling and breaking. "I'll say only this to you, girl; your world and Otherworld are linked closer than you dream, and if the powers of the dark overcome Andernesse, your world will not escape!"

Something moved in Ruth, answering his words independently of her will; suddenly she was looking sharply up into his face. "And closer than you too believe, Lord of the Hill of Assaroe," she heard herself saying, "for it is through humankind that Otherworld will be saved."

There was silence then, like a deep gasp. Ruth couldn't move, as if held inside the echo of her words. Her eyes seemed to have changed, seeing the half-mortals like giants made of pure light; she could feel a cold clear air in her face, and wondered if it was the wind in which they moved.

"Hear her!" Miach exclaimed.

Ilbrec turned away. "I'll hear nothing! Humans talk and talk, but there is only one of them who truly understands the battle we wage here against the dark – though we fight for their sake as much as ours! Back to your own world, girl, you and that white-faced boy

101

together!" His finger came towards them, pointing.

Light enveloped Ruth, a heatless blaze which seemed for an instant about to destroy her; and then she was gone into a great space of darkness. But then she was standing on sand again, with a grey mist all round her, and the melancholy cry of gulls echoing distantly.

She stood still, blind in the mist. All brightness and colour had gone, and it seemed possible that Ilbrec had sent her right out of the world, away into nothingness. He didn't believe me about Undry, she thought; he was too angry. He despises mortals ... Then there was a movement in the sand at her feet, and a voice spoke, hoarse and thin: "Ruth." It was Adam. She smelt the sea, mingled with the faint scents of grass and heath flowers, and then knew where she was: Starr Hills.

She knelt down by Adam. He sat hunched, his head bowed; then he looked up, and Ruth saw he was fully conscious again. Indeed, he had never looked so awake, all but shivering with awareness. But Ruth had to be sure. "Adam," she said.

His eyes reacted, coming to meet hers. He remembers who he is, Ruth thought with a pang of relief. But then Adam said, "Caer Wydyr," and his eyes stayed on her desperately.

"It's all right, Adam. We got you out of there ... " But Ruth's heart sank. It's not all right, she thought. Miach said no one could undo this spell.

"I've got to get back," said Adam, scrambling to his feet as if he couldn't bear to stay still. Ruth rose too, suddenly held by a despair more absolute than any she'd yet felt.

102

Adam stared round, and his head went up like a frightened horse's. "I can't stay here!"

"You must, Adam!" Ruth said urgently. "Fincara put a spell on you! It'll be worse if you go back!"

"No, it won't!" He stared at her, breathing in great gasps. "Don't you see? She's told me what I was born for – to bring her Undry. I know now what I'm meant to do!"

Ruth couldn't speak. This was worse than anything. All her fears had been of Adam dead, Adam never waking from his trance, Adam turned into an automaton. Not this. She saw his face changing as he remembered everything that had happened.

He thrust out a hand, pointing at her. "You took me out of Caer Wydyr!"

"Yes," said Ruth.

He cried out, a sound of pain and rage so inarticulate it was like a seagull's screech. "You bitch!"

"Adam—"

"Get away from me!" His face twisted with such hate that she almost stepped back. "You should have *killed* me! That wouldn't have hurt as much as – as coming back *here!*"

This couldn't be happening. "Adam," Ruth said again numbly, and reached a hand towards him.

He hit her, catching her so hard on the side of the head that she went down full-length on the sand. Without even waiting to see her fall he turned and ran, disappearing into the mist.

Ruth got up slowly, brushing the sand away. So cold she felt; cold, and heavy. It's as if I'm still under the sea,

103

she thought to herself – as if I'll always be there, whatever I do; deep down in the cold.

She had put one hand in the pocket of her waterproof to find a handkerchief, and she could feel something odd there. She brought it out: some dust and delicate fragments, creamy white and pink. Her head throbbed and there were stupid tears in her eyes; so it took her a while to realize that it was the shell Adam had given her.

Chapter 10

The rain had set in steadily by the time Ruth got home. She had found her shoes, stuck inside one of the pockets of her waterproof, and she supposed she probably looked quite normal. The cut on her brow seemed to have healed completely; Adam's had disappeared as well, she thought, remembering as best she could. Anyway, the people she met were all in a hurry, striding along with heads down in the rain, and no one appeared to notice her. Reaching the house, it wasn't until she was inside the porch that she realized Gran was there, standing on the doorstep and talking to someone.

Assuming it was one of the guests, she was about to mutter an excuse and go past; but then the man turned to her and said, "Well, Ruthie, love."

That stopped her short. She looked up – into a face she had once known very well.

Ben Hesketh. Jake had had no real friends except Ben; he had often been at the house in those old days, never saying much, but good at mending broken toys and constructing dolls out of handkerchiefs and folded paper. He had hardly changed – still the same bush of chestnut hair, meditative grey eyes and soft, hesitant voice. Ruthie.

No one but Jake and Ben Hesketh had ever called her that.

Now, just remembering made her feel shaky and babyish. "Hullo, Mr Hesketh," she said, and her voice nearly trembled.

"Nay, I'll think you've forgotten me," he said in his soft local accent. "You always called me Ben."

"Ben, I mean."

He looked at her, smiling slightly. But presently the smile faded, and Ruth thought he had seen something wrong in her face. She remembered he'd always been one for noticing things. But then Gran interposed.

"Well, you'll be back, Ben," she said rather irritably. "He's nobbut come to say he can't fetch that china away today, Ruth, love – his car's off the road. He can have a chat wi' you next time he comes. Go in, now, and get them sopping clothes off."

Ruth went in. Gran had always been tetchy and impatient with Ben Hesketh, she remembered; and he'd always called her Ma, as if he'd been Jake's brother. She realized, and it was a new thought, that he must have been very close to Jake ...

She heard him, now. "I'll be back tomorrow for the china, then, Ma. Now that other thing; if you change your mind, you know—"

"Nay," said Gran, and her voice was suddenly old – defeated, almost. "Take it away. I ne'er want to see that again."

Ruth heard no more, going swiftly through the house and down into the basement. Gran wouldn't follow her; her rheumatism was too bad to cope with the stairs more

106

than twice a day, morning and evening. Ruth left her waterproof in the bath to dry, and went into her room, shutting the door.

The room was exactly as she'd left it – shoes in the middle of the floor, the overall she wore for doing the bedrooms thrown over the back of the chair. The clock said twenty past three – about two hours, no more, after she'd left to go and find Adam on Starr Hills.

She stared at her face in the mirror. She wouldn't have been surprised to see her hair had all turned white; but it was the same face looking back at her. Not the same person, though; goodness knew what had happened to that person.

She sat down on her bed and wondered who she was now. "Gran, I'm not the normal one of the family after all; I'm a witch's daughter, I can travel to other worlds and make magic." I must be mad, she thought. But she didn't feel mad – just confused, terrified, changed. She sat there for nearly half an hour, staring at the wall, trying to get a grip. Presently there were feet on the stairs – a headlong clatter that would have frightened her had she been capable of ordinary feelings. Adam.

He came straight in without knocking, slammed the door behind him, and without a word began pulling the room to pieces. He jerked out drawers and scattered their contents on the floor, dragged all her clothes from the wardrobe, threw out her shoes, then pulled Ruth herself from the bed and ripped off the sheets. It was like watching a whirlwind. Ruth never thought of trying to stop him – not because she was afraid, but because he seemed unreachable now: beyond control or reason.

At last he turned to her, breathing hard, the room in a state of unbelievable chaos. *"Where is it?"* he shouted.

Ruth pressed her lips together. His face was white, stiff – *imprisoned*, she thought. He looked just like Fand, his real self locked away so that his body could do nothing but Fincara's commands. The mark of enchantment, Ruth thought. Of course he'd always been enchanted, but, before, it had been too deep in his mind to be fully felt; he'd only known there was something that kept him empty inside, stopped him from being a proper person. Now Fincara had filled that space, brought her spells into the centre of his mind, and he was aware of nothing else. Ruth shivered, wishing she didn't understand so perfectly, wishing she could hide it from herself.

"If you mean Undry," she said, "it was on the windowsill where you left it this morning. I saw it when I was doing the breakfasts. If it isn't there now, I don't know where it's gone, Adam."

He stared at her; and, minutely, his face changed. It was hardly more than a flicker in the eyes, but suddenly Ruth felt she glimpsed Adam again, her own brother, looking out at her desperately. She remembered he hadn't stayed under the chains in Caer Wydyr a night and a day, as Fincara had meant. Maybe she still had a chance with him.

She reached out and this time he let her grip his arm. "Don't hide it from me, Ruth!" he said huskily, and she knew he was pleading with her not to provoke a violence he could no longer control.

"Adam!" she said urgently. "I told you, I don't know where it is. But you can't take it back to *her*!"

108

She could sense the spells tightening on him, torment-
ing him. "I must. It's what I'm for," he said dully; but he
was still just there, looking through the bewitchment at
her. He said, "Where else could we take it, Ruth?"

She didn't know. She hesitated; and he gave a great
sigh and turned away, going heavily from the room.

"Well, what's it like to be back here after all this time,
Ruthie love?" Ben Hesketh asked. It was beginning to
rain, and he pressed the button for the windscreen
wipers.

Ruth looked ahead rather emptily. It was the following
day, a Tuesday; Ben Hesketh had arrived again, this time
with a big estate car, and Ruth had helped him load the
crates into the back. He had then suggested she come
with him to his house to help unload. She knew it was
only to talk to her; there was a yearning look in his eyes, a
look that was too young for the rest of his face.

"It's OK," she said. "A bit different, I suppose."

"Aye, it would be," Ben said in his gentle voice. "You're
different yourself, love. A grown woman now."

"Me?"

"Aye. Your Gran says. Busy and sensible as a woman
twice your age, she says. Doesn't know how she ever
managed wi'out you."

Ruth was silent. It was a cringe-making description at
the best of times; but now she knew it wasn't even true. No
one *really* sensible would have got into such a mess in
Otherworld – letting the panic take over and not even
trying to think straight. I work hard at dull, practical
things, she thought, and so everyone thinks I must be

109

mature and reliable and sensible; but really it's because I can't cope with the other things, the things that are frightening and dangerous.

These thoughts were so painful that she was glad to return to Ben's conversation. " 'Course, I ain't seen you since you left," he was saying. "Your Gran didn't want me around when you came visiting with Sarah and her family – wanted to have you to herself, she told me. So I'm fair staggered to see you so grown up."

"I don't think I'm really any different," said Ruth. Just as helpless and scared as when she was eight years old . . .

"Tell me, love," said Ben, "do you still miss your dad?"

His voice betrayed him; she saw at once it was Jake he wanted to talk about. She couldn't think what on earth to say. "I suppose I do," she said.

"I miss him all the time," said Ben quietly. "Beyond reason, I miss him."

Ruth looked at him sideways. His expression hadn't changed, but suddenly she saw an underlying loss and sadness, so much a part of him that it was easy to miss – but once seen, not easy to overlook again. Surely no one could look like that about Jake – her crazy, useless father?

"Most people in Wickrithe would say we were well rid of him," she said.

"Most people are wrong most of the time," he said, with such firmness that she slid him another look, surprised; he was strong behind his gentleness and hesitancy, she thought – strong in a way that wasn't common. She was beginning to see why he'd been Jake's friend.

"There's never been anyone like your dad, Ruthie," he said. "Those who called him crazy never knew him. When I was a little lad I had this mongrel puppy; he got summat wrong wi' him, and the vet wanted to put him down. Jake took him off me, kept him for a week, then brought him back, right as rain. I'd have done anything for your dad, ever since. Even then the kids were calling him Crazy Jake, and I don't know how many bloody noses I got in the playground, fighting to shut 'em up." He was silent, remembering. "See, love, your dad knew more than all the so-called sane people. Even when I couldn't rightly understand him, I always knew that at the heart of his talk there was summat good – summat true. Anyone could've seen that, if they'd bothered to listen. Folk never bother to listen, that's their trouble."

Ruth was silent. It was strange, the comfort she got from Ben's words, a sudden consoling warmth like finding an electric fire to turn on when the central heating failed in winter. *I always used to like him,* she remembered; *I was glad when he came to the house. I must have known somehow that he was the only person who didn't think Jake was crazy.*

The car drew up at one of the big houses on the prosperous shore road, facing the grassy slope that led up to the promenade. Ben Hesketh had clearly done well for himself out of his antiques business. Ruth could imagine him at salerooms, carefully handling dusty china, gently touching worn, cracked furniture, grey eyes seeming to question himself inwardly as he gazed; he would rarely fail, she thought, in spotting what was truly valuable. She got out, pulling up the hood of her waterproof, and helped him to carry the crates up the drive. He urged her to run into the house out of the rain and leave the work to him, but she declined; the crates were heavy and awkward for one person to handle, and after all it was what she'd come for.

"Well, you'll have to stay for a cup of tea, then," he said. "And I'm going to make it; I don't want you offering, thinking I'm helpless. You go and sit in the parlour."

The parlour was a big light room at the back of the house, with French windows leading to a garden. Ruth stood looking out. It was an old-fashioned kind of garden – beds of roses edged with white stones, and a high, mossy wall. The room was pleasant enough but had an unused, lonely feel. She guessed Ben lived mostly in the kitchen, cooking neatly and painstakingly for himself. She knew he'd never married.

It was when she turned away from the window that she saw it. Everything seemed to fade then, weirdly, leaving only one real object to stare at; and she went to the mantelpiece and took down from it Undry.

She realized she no longer had any doubts about this shabby metal cup. As she held it in her hands, it felt for a moment huge and heavy; light glimmered from it, and the sea sounded in her ears. For some reason she didn't understand, tears stung her eyes. Undry. But what was it doing here, in Ben Hesketh's house?

"So you've found that," a voice said, and Ruth looked blindly. It was Ben, with two mugs of tea on a tray. He smiled at her, told her to sit herself down, and held out a hand for Undry.

Ruth let him take it, and sat drinking her tea while he turned the cup over and over in his hands, gently and half

112

absentmindedly. "You'll have seen it before," he said.

"Yes," said Ruth, watching his hands. They had always been careful hands, and she sensed an extra reverence in them now. But Ben couldn't see what she seemed to be seeing – one moment a piece of shabby pewter, the next something that poured with sighing light.

"You hear of these stories," Ben said softly – making her wonder, briefly, if he did know what he held. "Old people bringing something out of the attic they've never cared for, and then seeing it fetch thousands of pounds at auction. Doesn't happen much, love, take my word. But if this is what I think it is, your Gran'll never have to worry about money again."

"What do you mean?" Ruth asked.

Ben went on turning the cup in his hands. "Funny I've never seen it before, the times I've been in your Gran's house," he said. "I just caught sight of it there on the kitchen windowsill, hiding amongst the plants. Where did that come from? I says. Ah, it's a thing Jake had from that woman he married, she says – like she didn't care for it. So I says, let me take it and get it valued, it could be worth a bit. Take it and get it out of my way, she says. And d'you know what I think, Ruthie?"

"What?" said Ruth.

Ben held it up. "Celtic, that engraving," he said, and his voice sank a little, awed. "Mind, I've never seen owt like it in the way of business, only in the books. It could be a fake, but I reckon not – you get to have a feel for what's real and what isn't, in this job. To my mind, it can't be later than fifth or sixth century – and if that's right, there won't be any price high enough."

113

Ruth was silent, her mind a queer turmoil. What she mainly felt was the sheer incongruity of talking about Undry in terms of salerooms and banknotes ... and at the same time, the impossibility of telling even Ben Hesketh the truth.

Ben looked at her, his eyes bright. "Don't say owt to your Gran, Ruthie; I've got to be sure first. I'm going over to Lancaster next week, and I've fixed to see an archaeologist chap at the university. If I'm right ... there'll be enough to take care of your Gran for the rest of her life, lovey. And that'll be a weight off my mind." His voice altered, wistfully. "Jake'd have wanted me to see her right; but she'll never take a penny piece off me ... "

Ruth knew Gran had refused money from Aunt Sarah and Uncle Nick. She couldn't think what to say. Money from the sale of an old cup that turned out to be valuable, that would be different; Gran would take it, without much thanks to Ben for his trouble, and perhaps it would be the end of all her struggles. She'd never retire; but she could fix up the house, put in some extra loos and bathrooms, have the kitchen completely refitted – get her business on a sound footing for the first time in her life.

"It'd be a grand thing, wouldn't it, Ruthie?" Ben said.

It would be a grand thing. Ruth looked at the cup in his hands, and two pictures presented themselves – Gran with all the anxiety gone from her face, and Undry full of light like the sea.

She put down her tea. "I think I'd better go back now, Ben," she said.

*

114

Disappointed, Ben drove her back. It had stopped raining, and she could easily have walked; but she let Ben drive her, slowly, talking about Jake all the way. She didn't know what to do. It had been like this ever since she and Adam had escaped from Otherworld; she seemed to have no strength left to decide anything. Often she was on the verge of tears for no reason, like a baby.

Aunt Sarah phoned that evening. Ruth heard Gran talking to her in the office – which was only a partitioned-off slice of the kitchen, so Ruth could hear every word as she stacked the dishwasher. But Gran wasn't giving anything away, just saying things like 'Aye' and 'Aye, well', and 'Not so bad'. Usually Aunt Sarah had a job to get a word in edgeways. And then after only five minutes Gran put down the phone and emerged, saying, "Ruth, lovey, come and have a word wi' your Aunt Sarah."

"Nothing's wrong, is it?" said Ruth, suddenly afraid. There seemed no limit now to what could go wrong; panic welled up in her at the least excuse.

"Nay, o' course not," said Gran testily. "Go on, now. I'm off to have a bath."

Ruth stared. "Now?" she queried. The dishwasher was only half-stacked, and the breakfast preparations not even started. Mornings were their times for baths.

"Aye. While the water's hot," said Gran firmly. She made a shooing gesture as Ruth, conscious that the water was always kept hot till midnight for the sake of the guests, continued to stare. "Come on, girl, quick. You haven't talked to your Aunt Sarah properly since you've been here."

Ruth twigged. Adam wasn't around, so she was getting

115

an opportunity for a confidential chat with Aunt Sarah. Which was kind of Gran; but as she went into the office and picked up the phone, she was aware of an unusual pang of nerves. The way things were, she was going to have to watch what she said to Aunt Sarah – and that was not something she'd had any practice in.

"Hullo, love." In the event, Aunt Sarah's voice was wonderfully steadying, bringing back the untidy, comfortable living room in Coniston with such vividness that Ruth could almost smell Uncle Nick's slippers scorching in front of the fire. Aunt Sarah would be curled up on the sofa, in guernsey and old jeans, having chased Robin and Jenny out so that she could phone in peace. "How are things?" Aunt Sarah asked.

Ruth occupied herself with getting settled on the office stool, aware that she couldn't speak until she'd swallowed the ridiculous tightness in her throat. *Honestly*. She was turning into such a crybaby . . . "All right," she managed. "I'm homesick, Aunt Sarah."

"Oh, poor old you. Well, we miss you too, you know. The house is a pigsty and no one's had a decent meal in days."

"Huh." Ruth felt better. "Might've known you wouldn't miss *me* – just my cooking and cleaning."

"No: we miss not having your funny face around to laugh at, too. Seriously, love, are you all right? I had your Gran on to me in a bit of a flap, saying she'd put her foot in it about your mother."

"Oh," said Ruth. "That." *Yes, Aunt Sarah, and since then I've remembered my mother's name, and the spell she put on me when I was a baby; and I've gone down to see her in her Castle under the sea . . .*

116

"You still there, love?" Aunt Sarah's voice was warm, remorseful. "I feel so bad about it. I should've talked to you about your mother long ago. I never realized you thought she was *dead*."

"I don't know why I did," Ruth said. It was still difficult to speak. "Gran says I used to turn away and not listen if anyone mentioned her."

"Yes, that's true, you did." Aunt Sarah sounded reflective. "It went very deep with you. I remember once I took you by the shoulders and said, 'Listen, love, I'm talking to you about your mother.' And you went the colour of rolled-out pastry and said, 'I feel sick, Aunt Sarah.' You were sick, too – you went running to the loo and threw up. You were really ill. I had to put you to bed."

"I don't remember that," said Ruth. She felt herself shivering.

"I do." Aunt Sarah sighed. "When you came to us, love, you were eight years old and you never smiled, you never laughed, you hardly said anything. So when you showed us you didn't want to hear about your mother, we thought – well, we thought we'd better go along with you. We decided we wouldn't mention her till you did of your own accord. Which of course you never did. It's my fault; I should've made sure we talked about her, once you were older. But I suppose by then I'd got into the habit of never mentioning her."

"Yes, I see," said Ruth. "It doesn't matter, Aunt Sarah."

"It does matter, love. She's your mother."

From thy mother, in Undersea, witch's power comes to thee . . . Ruth closed her eyes. She could understand her eight-year-old self, sick with terror at the mere mention of

117

Fincara. I haven't grown up at all, she thought hopelessly.

"Ruth, love? Still there?"

"Yes," said Ruth. "I still don't really want to talk about her, Aunt Sarah."

"Hmm." Aunt Sarah, not usually the worrying type, didn't sound happy. "Well, all right, I won't nag. It's not as if I could tell you much, anyway, seeing I never met her."

"Didn't you?" Ruth was surprised. "Never?"

"Well, she wasn't around for very long. Just a couple of years, long enough to have you and Adam. I was having Rob and Jen at the same time, and I used to get very wrapped up in myself when I was pregnant, you know – just not interested in things like sisters-in-law. But that wasn't the main reason. For a good five years, round then, I wasn't speaking to your dad, or your Gran."

"Not *speaking* to them?" That came as total news to Ruth. "Why not?"

"Oh . . . " Aunt Sarah sounded wry. "I was young, just into my twenties, and in a silly phase. I hated Wickrithe and everything in it. I thought Gran and Jake had ruined my childhood, Jake because he wasn't like other boys and Gran because to my mind she wouldn't do enough about him. So I decided I wasn't going to have any more to do with them."

Ruth was silent, as stunned as if a bus had driven into her. She'd known Aunt Sarah had a temper, but to stay in a temper for *five years* . . . Suddenly it felt dark and oppressive in the little office, heavy with all the unhappiness there'd ever been in the Demdyke house. Poor Aunt Sarah, Ruth thought. Poor Gran.

She said, "It doesn't sound a bit like you, Aunt Sarah."

Aunt Sarah chuckled ruefully. "Oh, don't think you know everything about me, my girl. I've been a right so-and-so in my time."

"When did you start talking to them again?"

"When I got around to realizing how I'd feel if Rob or Jenny ever refused to have anything to do with me. Obvious, really. But I wasn't very sensible when I was younger, love. Not like you."

Ruth felt herself stiffen. "I'm beginning to get so fed up with people calling me sensible, Aunt Sarah."

"But you *are*," said Aunt Sarah. "Sensible. Reliable. Such a help to everyone. That's what your guide captain said to me once – or was it Mrs Tyson at the riding stables? One of those people. And why ever shouldn't you be pleased, love? No one would say that about Rob or Jen. Or me, come to that."

"But it isn't really true. There are lots of things I'm not sensible about."

"What things?"

Ruth swallowed. Being captured by warriors from Otherworld; being taken over by her own magic. It was scarcely bearable, talking to Aunt Sarah with this invisible wall between them of things that couldn't be mentioned. I've never stopped myself talking to her about anything before, she thought. But that wasn't true; she remembered her mother.

She said at last, "Adam."

"Oh, *Adam*. Well, love, all I can say about Adam is that he's Jake all over again – and being sensible never got anyone anywhere with Jake. *Un*common sense is what you need with those two."

"What was Jake like?" Ruth asked. "Why wasn't he the same as other boys?"

Aunt Sarah sighed. "He was sweet to me when I was small. He was only a year older, but sort of *fatherly*. Very gentle – he never got into fights, with me or anyone else; and he'd play with me for hours. I adored him, love, I really did. But as we got older it got harder and harder to talk to him; he seemed to withdraw. He used to go off on his own and come back in a sort of daze, as if he couldn't understand anything we said to him. I hated that. I just couldn't cope with it. It was as if he'd gone into a different world."

"It's like that with Adam," said Ruth. "Except he doesn't seem to be in any sort of world. You can't *find* him. And he can't find himself either."

"Oh, love."

"And he gets angry. He gets scared, and that makes him angry." Ruth touched her temple, feeling the bruise where Adam had hit her. "He thinks so much about our parents, Aunt Sarah. I just don't know what's going to happen to him . . . " She stopped, aware that all the craziness had nearly overflowed then. *He's under a spell, Aunt Sarah. A spell our mother laid on him.*

"Oh, love," said Aunt Sarah again. "It's all getting too much for you, isn't it?"

Ruth bit her lips, struggling to calm down. "No," she said. "I'm all right. Honestly."

"Look, love, if you'd like to give it all up and come home, don't be too proud to say so." Aunt Sarah hesitated, uncharacteristically, and her tone altered a little. "Actually, Ruth love, I'd like you to come home. I seem to've had bad vibes about you lately. I don't know if it's just that I'm missing you . . . I feel something's *wrong*. Shall I come down in the car for you tomorrow?"

Ruth was silent, gripping the phone in both hands so hard that a dull ache started up. Oh, *yes* – the thought of escaping back to Coniston was so utterly desirable that she had a job not to rush off and start packing her case. But her feelings faltered, and then divided chillingly – for she'd changed, and who knew if Coniston would be the same for her now? She thought of going back and finding it all different, the old contentment shattered . . . and she knew she couldn't bear that. I don't know what I want, she thought. I don't know what to do at all.

She said, "I couldn't, really. Gran can't manage on her own."

"She'll have to when your holidays are over, won't she? And surely Adam can do a bit to help."

"No; he's really no use. But she won't be so busy when the summer's over. She doesn't get many people in the off-season."

Aunt Sarah sighed. "Well, I promised your Uncle Nick I wouldn't do any persuading. He says we ought to let you stick it out if you want to. But we're here, love, if you want us. All you have to do is phone, and I'll be straight down to fetch you. Like a shot."

"Thanks, Aunt Sarah," said Ruth, knowing her boats were now completely burnt. Perversely, she felt nearer to tears than at any other moment in the conversation – a great anguishing flood of tears, as if for something that was lost and would never come again. *I want my home*, she thought, and was appalled by her childishness; but the tide of emotion was irresistible, surging through her like great waves. She had to swallow hard, and study the calendar opposite with meticulous care, to avoid actual tears. She asked for news of Robin and Jenny, and Aunt Sarah launched into an ironic description of how a Japanese tourist half Jenny's size and four times her age had proposed marriage to her ("At least I *hope* it was marriage"), and how Robin had got locked overnight in the bar of the hotel where he was working and had taken two days to sleep it off; and gradually Ruth fought down her feelings. She sat listening, bruised and exhausted.

Presently they hung up, but Ruth went on sitting there, staring at the guest register, the typewriter, the neat stacks of envelopes and headed notepaper. It was the first time she'd ever spoken to Aunt Sarah and come away with this feeling of no comfort, no help, weighing her down as if the big brass door stop from the porch had got lodged inside her. I've changed so much, she thought; I'm a person I don't know any more.

She dreamed of Fincara that night, fierce laughter ringing in her ears, magic binding her like a cold sticky web; and woke just before dawn, too afraid even to cry. She put on her bedside lamp, and that helped a little. Undry was in her mind, shedding troubled surges of light through deep darkness; what am I going to *do*? she wondered, and knew it was beyond her to decide anything. I promised Fand I'd bring her Undry, she thought; but even Fand said she didn't think it would do

122

any good ... and there's no point thinking about it because I just *can't*. Let Ben take it to the man in Lancaster. Let him sell it off to a museum. Once it's locked up inside a glass case, surely it's safe; no one can expect me to do anything about it then.

Chapter 11

Gran usually made tea at ten o'clock, when the evening meal was cleared away and everything ready for next morning's breakfasts. But on Thursday night she sat in her chair, the pain-lines deep in her face, and presently Ruth got up and filled the kettle.

"Like your rug over your knees, Gran?" she asked, knowing it helped when her rheumatism was bad.

"Aye," said Gran wearily. "And draw the curtains and put the light on, lass. It's that miserable outside..."

Ruth obeyed, shutting out the rainy evening. She switched on the wall light over the table rather than the bright central strip, hoping it would look cosier; but it only seemed to bring up the shadows. Adam sat motionless in one of the corners – looking less and less like a real person, Ruth noted; he never spoke now, or appeared to hear if anyone addressed him. He seemed so fiercely shut up in himself that Ruth was afraid people would start seriously meaning it when they called him mad.

She brought the tartan rug and Gran, uncharacteristically passive, allowed it to be tucked round her legs. "Hark to that rain," she muttered.

"Won't it ever stop?" said Ruth.

"Not before there's a flood. You mark my words, lass . . . "

The kettle boiled and Ruth made the tea, wondering if Gran was right. The wind was getting up, too – they heard it bluster round the house, flinging rain on the windows. Ruth shivered; her spirits were low enough without this.

"Sometimes it all comes to a head," Gran said, low, and shut her eyes while the pain furrowed her face. "It were a night like this when your mother went off, lass, and Jake near lost his mind when he knew she'd gone for good. That's past, now; yet there's naught better coming. Here I am, after all I've worked and striven for – with Jake the Lord knows where; my strength failing; and that poor lad there in the corner . . . "

Ruth looked at Adam, but he gave no sign of having heard. "Gran!" she whispered, and knelt down beside her, squeezing her hand. "You've got me and Aunt Sarah and everyone too."

Gran sighed, and the wind came again, rushing round the house with a noise like women's voices wailing. In the middle of it, the latch rattled, and hair prickled on Ruth's neck. The door opened quietly; and stepping into the kitchen, as he had stepped a thousand times before, came Jake.

He closed the door and advanced into the middle of the room. To Ruth, crouching by Gran, he seemed hugely tall; but he gazed round like a helpless child, seeming not to see them at first. Drops of rain clung to his hair, sparkling. For a moment Ruth wondered if he were real or just a ghost.

Gran's eyes opened, sudden and sharp. "Jake," she said under her breath, "where do you come from?"

He turned to her, but not as if he knew who she was. "I've been in a dark place," he murmured. "The place between the worlds, where you feel the edges of them grind and shatter. Ah...why can they not all be one?"

Ruth had never heard him sound much madder. Gran sighed, bitterly. "Is that all you've to say to me?" she demanded. "Nay, you've not come for my sake – that's clear. There's your boy: there in the corner. You left him for me to tend, with never a word, and I've done my best for him. There he is, Jake: waiting for you."

Ruth looked, and saw Adam had at last reacted to something; he was crouched low in his corner, eyes set on Jake. The two faces, so alike, gazed at each other.

Jake stepped towards Adam, and held out his hands. "Adam, lad, come now, and bring Undry."

Adam just stared, fiercely.

"Come on, son." Jake's voice grew urgent. "There's little time left. All these years, I never knew that cup was Undry! I should have told you, the night I met you on Starr Hills; but I'd only that day realized and I was afraid who might be listening. Even the half-mortals don't know – they still think Undry's lost, or in the hands of the dark powers. We must take it to them, lad. They're the only ones in all the worlds who can keep it safe now!"

Still Adam stared, grimmer than shouts or blows. Ruth shivered.

"Adam!" Jake's palms turned upwards in entreaty. "It's a thing greater than anyone's life – don't you know? Please, lad, please!"

126

Adam rose. "I haven't got it," he said, and it was so long since he'd last spoken that the first words came hoarse and harsh, like the sound of some animal. "I brought it to Starr Hills for you but you ran away from me without even looking round! Now it's gone!"

Jake's hands fell. "I couldn't wait for you, boy. The Women were coming, with their spears."

"They came after me with their spears, too!" Ruth heard Adam's teeth grit at the memory. "I've been down under the sea, you know! I've been to Fincara's Isle and spoken to her!"

It was Jake who stared now, his face going still with horror. There was a long silence, as if he were so fixed in despair he couldn't speak. "Adam," he whispered at last, "Adam – boy – remember yourself! I know the spells laid on you at your birth, for I heard her sing them – and I smiled, may I be forgiven, for I thought then I'd have the strength to break them! I know now what her power is – strong enough to shatter a man's mind and cast him from this world. But she can never entirely master a human soul – not unless you consent to it! Remember who you are, Adam – remember your own self!"

"I have remembered!" Adam shouted at him. "I was born to bring her Undry, and that's all I ever shall do! Let me alone! You knew when I was born what would happen to me!"

They were both silent, gazing at each other, Jake's face aghast. Then Adam pushed past him, out of the kitchen door, slamming it. After a moment Ruth heard the thud of the garden gate closing.

For a moment, no one moved or spoke. Then Gran said thinly, "Ah, Jake. You see now how it is when your child's wits fail, and there's naught you can do for him. You see now!"

Jake stood as if he carried a brimming cup which the slightest motion could spill. But Ruth sensed he wanted to speak, and was struggling through pain and craziness to do so.

"It's true," he whispered at last, carefully. "I'm not in my right mind; but don't let that hurt you! How could a man be sane who has to live as I do, hunting across the worlds for safety? I'm only a man, yet I have to live like one of the half-mortals! And it's the same for the boy; I thought I could keep him from it, but I see now I can't. It's I who've brought him to this! Yet that's as it must be; don't let it trouble you ..."

Ruth looked into his strange shaken eyes. She had no idea what he meant, and if she tried to answer she knew she'd only cry. Oh, Jake ...

It was Gran who answered, stronger than Ruth despite everything. "Find rest, Jake," she said, low. "Find rest."

It was totally silent in the kitchen; Ruth could hear the wind and slashing rain outside, and, upstairs, one of the guests moving about; but in the room itself time seemed to have stopped. Jake had turned away towards the shadows, standing with bent head and closed eyes.

"Ilbrec!" he whispered at last. "Let me come back!"

Ruth's heart stood still. *Ilbrec* ... The wind rose in a rending sigh, filling the night with sound, and slowly sank again to quietness. Ilbrec's voice came then – not the thundering voice she remembered, but low, fading like sorrow: "Jacob, come, come. For we've sore need of you."

128

Jake's head lifted sharply. But he stood for a moment, hesitating, and Ruth saw a look of such sadness go over his face that tears threatened her again. Then, with one slow glance back at them, he turned to the door, opened it, and went out. It shut behind him.

No other sound followed – until Gran raised her hands to her cheeks and began to moan softly. Ruth tried to put her arms round her, but with sudden firmness Gran pushed her away. "Go to your brother, lovey," she whispered. "Go to your brother. Quick, now."

Outside, the garden was empty; but Ruth found Adam where she'd expected, under the big chestnut tree that grew at the end of the lane. For the first time in days his eyes seemed to acknowledge her. The tree had been another meeting place of their childhood, and she knew the flaky bark and cracked pavement by heart. Somehow the familiarity calmed her.

"Adam," she said, "we've got to give Undry back to Jake."

Adam went on looking at her, and her heart sank; perhaps he'd gone too far away in his mind to come back now. "Adam—" she said.

"I heard you," said Adam – in his harsh, not-quite-human voice. "But I have to take Undry where it belongs."

"It belongs with Jake, Adam!" This certainty had somehow emerged from her indecision. "He's gone to Andernesse; that's the only safe place there is now. Undry won't be safe anywhere else. Adam, we've *got* to!"

He just looked at her. "Where is it?" he said.

Ruth swallowed. She should have known she couldn't

129

forget Undry and hope everything would just stop. Undry wouldn't let her. But if I can get it to Andernesse somehow, she thought, then surely it'll be safe and everything *will* stop . . . "It's in Ben Hesketh's house," she said. "Gran gave it to him."

Adam turned at once and set off through the rain. Ruth hurried after him, her heart going in great jolts; the rain came down bewilderingly, making it difficult to know where they were. She thought of Fand, briefly, but the thought broke up in confusion.

When Adam stopped, she saw they'd reached a lane running between the backs of houses. High garden walls bordered it on both sides. Adam lifted the latch on one of the gates and pushed it with great care; but it didn't move, obviously bolted.

Ruth tried to get her breath. Wet through now, she felt cold and queer, as if she were starting an illness. And there was something wrong with the weather; the rain streamed, but not steadily, and the sky seemed full of noise and disturbances, like great clouds battling. One thing was clear, though, from that stealthiness of Adam's: he hadn't come here to *ask* Ben Hesketh for the cup.

"Adam—" she gasped.

He made a sharp shushing gesture. "It's Thursday, isn't it?" he whispered, and it was strange to hear him say something so ordinary. "He'll be out at the Rotary Club dinner. Give me a hand up."

Ruth found herself giving him a shove as he jumped for the top of the gate. He gripped it with his hands, got his foot on to the latch, heaved up and rolled over the top. She heard him drop quietly on the other side, and draw

130

the bolt. The door opened, and he gripped her wrist and pulled her through.

It was Ben Hesketh's garden; she saw the roses. The stones edging the flower beds were dark now with rain.

Adam closed the gate softly. "Where is it?" he hissed.

Ruth was shaking, not with fear so much as protest; she'd lost control of this situation. She remembered how helplessly she'd given way to Jake's madness on Starr Hills. "In the room with the French windows," she heard herself answer. "But *Adam*—"

"Quiet." Still gripping her wrist, he led her over to the French windows. He bent to look at the fastening, then picked up one of the white stones and struck; the glass tinkled thinly, a horrible sound. He slid his hand through the hole, flicked back the catch, and swung the window open. "Come on," he whispered.

Ruth entered with him, shivering. No burglar alarm; either Ben didn't have one, or, uncharacteristically careless, he'd left it switched off. But what if Undry wasn't here? What if Ben had left it with the man in Lancaster? What if he came back and caught them now?

Then she saw it. It was on the mantelpiece, as before, and its light flowed round it like water. She saw it had woken further into its power, for the light was visible, washing through the dark; it sighed like the sea. She saw Adam take two strides to it and grip it in his hands.

Then the sirens began.

They were distant at first, but though they came nearer, neither she nor Adam moved. Then they swept past with

131

a great roar of engines, and there seemed to be a voice shouting from a loudspeaker. It sounded like some huge vehicle; a fire engine, maybe. Ruth had thought it was the police coming after them and, stupidly, she relaxed.

Then she saw the water. It came as if Undry had called it, slipping under the door and pooling on the carpet. She heard Adam gasp, and panic went through her like an electric shock.

The front door burst open. They heard Ben Hesketh's voice – "Oh, my God!" He was on them before they could move, blundering down the hall and flinging the door wide. They saw him stare, his face already horrified – then he shouted, incomprehensibly, "Come on! Upstairs, quick!"

Adam struck. In a single movement, he had snatched a vase from the mantelpiece and brought it smashing against Ben's temple, as neat as the stone through the French window. Ben dropped where he stood, his hand splashing into one of the pools. "*Adam!*" Ruth screamed.

He seized her and thrust her outside. Out there in the rain, she could hear the sirens still howling, and great voices echoing; blue and red lights, flashing, skidded across the undersides of clouds. Ruth felt as if she were breaking inside.

"Come on!" Adam cried and, gripping Undry in both hands, he crashed through the garden gate and began to run.

Ruth ran after him, horror building and building; but she couldn't catch him up. He turned down a street leading to the coast road, and Ruth knew he was heading for Starr Hills. She pounded after him desperately; she could still see him, though daylight had all but died. It was several moments before she realized she was running ankle-deep in water.

She reached the coast road and a fire engine charged into view, spreading a bow wave. One of the loudspeaker voices was talking, a huge, curiously calm voice: "Do not leave your homes. Go to the top floor of your house and remain there till the water goes down ... " A man in the cab leaned out and shouted something at her as the fire engine churned past, but she couldn't hear what.

She had to stop a few yards later, sobbing for breath. The water swirled cold round her feet, and she had lost sight of Adam. She heard a sash window go up, and turned to look; it was a first-floor window, and a woman was leaning out to her.

"Do you live close, dear?" she called. "Because if so, for heaven's sake go straight home."

Ruth got her breath back, and her mind began to function again, slowly. "Is the river flooding?" she asked.

"Yes; it's coming in by Copers Bakery. There's a warning on local radio that it'll soon be over Starr Hills as well."

Starr Hills ... And she *knew* that was where Adam had gone. Ruth stood shaking with despair and indecision; I can't cope, she thought, I've gone to pieces like I always do ...

"Look, dear," the woman called to her. "If you don't live close, you'd better come in and share our top floor. The water's rising very fast, they say."

133

But I've no choice, Ruth thought desperately; I can't leave Adam. I daren't, not now he's got Undry. "It's all right," she called. "I can easily get home. Thank you."

"Are you *sure*?" The woman sounded doubtful; but Ruth set off, running purposefully, and didn't look back. She could picture the flood in her mind, coming up the bed of the Liggard and spreading out behind the sea wall. The road was a river already. She didn't have much time.

Soon she was off the road, clambering over the hummocks of Starr Hills. The ground was comparatively dry, and she guessed the sea would be checked for a while by the dunes; but not for long. "Adam!" she called, but was too breathless for her voice to carry. She stopped, gasping; and then, through the rush and thunder of the storm, a faint reply seemed to come.

"Mortal . . . "

Cold came spreading through her from head to foot, slowly; she felt it in her lips most, an unnatural iciness. Oh *no*, she thought – as if she'd known all along this was what would happen. Next moment she was blundering towards the voice, blindly, hardly noticing when she stumbled; she came to the hollow where the wrecked car lay, and saw a pale patch on the ground beside it. So faint, it might only be moonlight through the clouds – then she saw long pale hair streaming.

She wasn't sure if she cried out. Somehow she scrambled down into the hollow and landed on her knees by Fand. She couldn't speak. The Woman seemed less than a ghost, just a shape lying. But then she opened her eyes, and her face was clear and still; Ruth saw the enchantment on her was at an end. Everything, now, was at an end for Fand.

"Mortal," she whispered. The rain had darkened her hair, but it still seemed to float around her. "Oh, mortal, who will help you now? Fincara has cast me out of Undersea for my treachery; and now I am dying."

Ruth took her hand, gripping. She'd known this would happen, but she'd done nothing; she'd never done anything for Fand.

The Woman was fading away – melting into the darkness of Starr Hills. She looked up at Ruth, her face transparent, almost colourless; but her eyes were as deep as the sea. "Would I could have lived to see you freed from her spells, mortal!" she whispered. "Now you must free yourself. Do not let her win . . . "

Still Ruth couldn't speak. I could have brought her Undry so easily, she thought; but I left it at Ben Hesketh's . . . and then told Adam we should take it to Andernesse . . . She gripped Fand almost roughly, as if she could hold her back from dying. Then a movement caught her eye, and she looked to see Adam coming warily round the car, Undry in his hands.

Her voice came back. "Adam!" she screamed, reached out and caught him by the sleeve.

He gasped. "Let go!" He pulled away, but Ruth's hand closed desperately, not daring to lose him again. Savagely, he turned on her, and hit out with the rim of Undry.

Though the blow didn't strike Ruth, it seemed to. Without any warning the great wave came crashing, obliterating everything; she knew she was crying out,

135

shouting words of furious magic; but all she could feel was Fand's hand in hers. The sea answered her voice, and she saw a great heave of water rise and fling itself over the dunes. But that was far away; very far away. She closed her eyes and gripped the cold hand.

When she opened them again, she was where she expected to be. A golden sun filled the air with light, and green sea lapped the sand. Wind stirred with a wordless hushing in the Forest of Andernesse.

Adam was there, the violence draining from him as he stared round. Ruth stayed still, kneeling on the yellow shore, and presently let go of Fand's dead hand.

Chapter 12

As she knelt there, with Fand lying quietly before her on the beach, nothing else seemed to matter much. Adam looked ashen, sick, gripping Undry as if his life depended on it; and Ruth knew he'd almost killed her just then. But that wasn't important. Nothing was important. She supposed what she felt was partly the deadness that always followed her magic, but this time there was more. Much more. Even when she looked up and saw the half-mortals approaching from the forest, she hadn't the strength to be afraid.

And in fact they seemed more human, less terrifying than before. Their faces were sombre, holding no anger. They came on to the golden sand and stood in silence, winds of light moving over them plainly, despite the brightness of the evening sunshine.

Then Ilbrec spoke as if to one of his own kind, in a great voice full of echoes. "Again you have come, Fincara's daughter, and again you bring us naught but sorrow. Give me the Lady Fand, that I may bear her to a fitting place."

Ruth instinctively clasped Fand's hand again; she'd taken it for granted the half-mortals would be hostile to one of Fincara's Women. But looking up at Ilbrec she saw such a heartbroken sorrow that without a word she let him stoop and take Fand from her. What was this? Why should Ilbrec grieve for poor Fand?

"Come," said Ilbrec, holding the Woman in his arms. "Bring Undry, boy."

The half-mortals followed him, going back into the Forest. Adam went with them, carrying Undry; the Cauldron looked silvery now and by moments the light washing from it was plain to see. Ruth put her face in her hands and listened to them go, hoping perhaps everyone would forget her now.

But presently a quiet voice said, "Ruthie."

She lifted her head, startled. A big broad-shouldered man stood there, looking gently down at her; he seemed almost as tall as the half-mortals, his shadow streaming a long way across the beach. "Jake," Ruth whispered. She'd forgotten he'd come here ahead of them.

She got up, gazing at him; for this seemed not the crazy figure of recent days, but Jake as she remembered him from years ago, her own father. She examined him hard, trying to decide what it was that had changed; the wind was freshening off the sea, lifting the dark hair from his brow, and his face looked strong, serene. "You – know who I am, now?" she said uncertainly.

His eyes softened. "I always knew, child. Even when I seemed crazy: even on Starr Hills. How could I not? Whatever changes come to you, whatever in the world happens, you're my daughter."

Ruth found herself in his arms, her face against his broad chest – as if she were a little girl again, in the time

138

before she'd known he was crazy. She hadn't realized she remembered that time. It was like a place to hide in, a great strong haven holding her ... but she knew she couldn't stay there. I'm too changed, she thought; too much has happened. She raised her head and looked into his eyes. It was strange how wise those eyes looked, here in Andernesse.

"Jake," she said hesitantly, "you're different."

He smiled, a little sadly. "This is Otherworld, Ruthie. I found the way here when I was a boy, and it spoils you for the human world. I've been a poor father to you. But by the time you were born I couldn't give up Otherworld; I was deep in the battle we wage here against the powers of the dark, and to leave it would have been deserting. When I went, seven years ago, it was to fight harder in the battle. My thoughts were all on that. But they don't understand such things in the human world; and I understand their world less and less. When I go back there, my mind grows confused; I seem a madman, no use to anyone."

He didn't seem mad now. Ruth remembered Ben: *your dad knew more than all the so-called sane people ...*

"I thought you went to find Fincara," she said.

"So I did, in part," he said, and a shadow went over him. "But she hid herself well. It was not till nine days ago that at last I found her, and saw what she was doing on her isle." His voice sank. "That's a fearful place, Ruthie! I had on the Ring of Luned that brings invisibility, and I saw the Glass Castle and the chains hanging in the Great Tower. And then I realized that the little cup she'd brought with her out of the sea, and gave to me for Adam – that little cup could be none other than Undry." He was silent, and Ruth felt him shiver with the memory. "Ah, Ruthie – it's for the boy I grieve."

Adam. "But there was nothing anyone could have done," said Ruth.

"No. She laid her spells too well. Yet if I'd known then that the cup was Undry . . . I gave it to you, knowing you were stronger than him, for you had her magic; I thought perhaps you'd keep his destiny from him. Yet I should have known. I heard her set the spells on him. I should have known nothing could break them."

Ruth was silent, Adam's spellbound face very clear in her mind's eye.

"Ah, child," Jake whispered, "there's so much to regret in what I let happen to him. And you, too."

"But surely it's all right now, isn't it?" Ruth said slowly. "Undry's safe, now?"

Jake hesitated. "Look," he said at last, turning to the sea. "You've eyes that can see such things, Ruthie. There's the spell-wall."

Ruth looked doubtfully out to sea, wondering what he meant; but then she began to see something, more with her mind's eye than in reality, though she knew at once it was very real. It was like a wall of crystal a thousand feet high, rising from the sea not far from the shore – strong, massive, yet as fine as spun glass. Ruth saw now why Andernesse was as it was; everything dark or evil was kept out behind that soaring wall. The greatness of the magic awed her.

"I see it," she said.

"Look beyond. What do you see outside?"

"Darkness," said Ruth after a moment. "Shadows . . . "

140

She turned away sharply, afraid of what might emerge from that vague hosting of blackness. "What is it, Jake?"

"Shadows and darkness," said Jake sombrely. "The power of the dark. It has been gathering there ever since the breach was healed. And we have Undry now – we have all four Treasures safely held. Yet still the darkness gathers."

Ruth's throat tightened. "What can we do?"

He turned his head, looking down at her gently. "Ah, Ruthie – you're so afraid, child. You must get beyond the fear. For we need your strength now, more than anyone's."

They stood in silence, while the sun dipped in the west. And Ruth felt she hadn't understood till now what it meant, to be Jake's daughter; she'd never guessed that one day he would turn to her like this, calling her to understand all the past and set her own strength beside his. Yet what strength did she have for him? *This my spell on you is laid: you'll be always too afraid . . .* What could *she* do?

"Come," said Jake at last. "We must go to Kilgrimol Hill."

Kilgrimol was inland, a green hill standing above the forest. As they walked amidst the great trees, Ruth seemed to wake at last from the deadness that had possessed her since arriving in Andernesse. Leaves murmured, and foxglove and mallow nodded by the path; and a butterfly glinted past like a flake of amber. The trees shed a radiance of their own, turning the air green and gold; and Ruth felt that if only she could escape alone into those dreaming glades, all the despair and dread would be lifted from her. Yet it was a feeling of deep pain, as if she'd come too late, as if the chance had gone and would never come again. She didn't understand her feelings. I never do, she thought.

The summit of Kilgrimol was almost level, bearing only a small round building of stone with a high peak of thatch. Reaching the top, Ruth looked eastward; she could see beyond the forest to purple hills and faint mountains. *If only*, she thought; but it was no good wishing, especially when she didn't even know what she was wishing for. She watched the swallows that had begun to fly over the hill in the last of the light; they skimmed close, almost round her feet.

"Come," said Jake, "we must go into the Treasure House."

The Treasure House was cool and dim, with only the doorway and one small window to admit the light. Ilbrec stood there, and Adam beside him, still holding Undry. The floor was of bare earth, and a ring of wooden poles supported the roof. By the central pole stood a great oaken chest, three feet high and as long as a man. Fand lay on it, her hair spread over the dark wood. At her right hand was an ancient sword, its blade grey and pitted; at her left, a bronze spear, worn smooth with age; and at her feet, an unshaped granite stone.

"Ilbrec," said Jake, his voice resounding in the small space. Ilbrec turned to him, his light plain in the dim room, and then they gripped each other in their arms, Ilbrec hiding his face on Jake's shoulder. So they stood, quite still; and Ruth saw that Jake was not, like her, a mere mortal amongst half-mortals, but Ilbrec's equal; and as they drew apart, looking deeply into each other's faces, she saw too that he was Ilbrec's dearest friend. That shook her to her heart; she'd known he was different from other men, but not this different.

"This is the most honourable place I may lay her," Ilbrec said, low. "Here with Nuada's Sword from the City of Findias; the Ildana's Spear from Gorias; and the Stone of Fate from Falias. For it is here that all our strength lies, the last certainty that light may survive in darkness. Two thousand years we have kept these three Treasures safe here. For if they are used amiss, all our power would end; the spell-wall would break, the dark would come in on us." He paused, looking directly at Ruth. "Do you understand me, Fincara's daughter? Do you know what these Treasures are, and the Cities I speak of?"

"Yes," said Ruth slowly. Things were becoming clear; she remembered what Miach had told her, and, before that, Fincara. "Once there were four Cities, in the north, south, east and west; and each City had its own Treasure, to guard against the dark."

"So it was," said Ilbrec. "So it was, long ago. But then the dark powers rose, and the four Cities fell; it was the most we could do to save the Treasures. It was I who brought the Ildana's Spear, fleeing from Gorias."

Jake spoke; his voice was different, deeper and more echoing, as if he spoke in the language of the half-mortals. "Tell my children how that was, Ilbrec, to let them learn the powers of our enemy."

Evening light was slanting through the doorway, setting a sheen in the ancient spear-head. But it was the

143

coming night that seemed to press down on Ruth; there was a strange fear in her that the sun, if it sank this evening, might never rise again. She didn't want Ilbrec to speak.

"It is not a good memory, Jacob," he said, bleakly. "The dark had descended on us in a howling storm, as it will when the world ends. Perhaps, if we had only tried to wield the Spear, we would have been saved; but none had the heart or the courage. This is the great power of the dark, Jacob, that it takes away our steadfastness and trust in ourselves. I was bidden take the Spear and escape. And as I fled I looked back and saw Gorias die into the dark behind me; the gold towers of Paradise sank like fading flames."

Adam stirred suddenly beside Ruth; she saw him lift his white face. "Paradise?" he said hoarsely.

"Yes. Gorias was the last of the Cities to fall, and even mortals remember it. It became mingled with the tales of a folk who lived in the east of your world; they called it Adam's Paradise."

Jake turned and looked urgently at his son; but Adam's gaze had fallen back to Undry, and Ruth wasn't sure he'd heard. Herself, she felt only the irony; hell was nearer Adam's experience than paradise.

Ilbrec spoke again. "Do you know which City Undry comes from, Fincara's daughter?"

She looked at the Cauldron, small and ancient as the other Treasures. "From the City of the West," she said. "Murias – the Crystal Isle. And the Crystal Isle must be the same as the Glass Castle: Caer Wydyr."

Ilbrec's voice deepened. "What else do you know of Caer Wydyr?"

Ruth could feel herself shivering, just at the name. "Fincara's trying to bring back Murias. She's half brought it back already, but she can't make it more than a ruin. That's why she wants Undry – to bring it back properly."

"Ah!" Ilbrec breathed, and his eyes lit fiercely. "So Fincara would be mistress of Murias, would she? Then indeed the dark powers would conquer!"

"That's why we've brought Undry here," Ruth said. "This is the only safe place for it."

Ilbrec was silent at that, and Ruth looked at him with a quick tightening of anxiety. He had turned to regard Undry, and his face looked worn, old.

"Safe?" he said at last, very quietly. "When Murias fell, it was my brother Gaiar who saved Undry and carried it to Andernesse. With great reverence we laid it here in the Treasure House. And yet . . . there was a night, long ago now, when a mist came in off the sea; we slept uneasily, then woke in the dark, to hear the cold whine of sea-magic in the air. We seized our weapons and ran to Kilgrimol, and out of the Treasure House came a band of warrior women, bearing Undry. They had helmets of silver and spears like flames. Ah . . . !" Ilbrec closed his eyes momentarily. "Many battles have I fought, but it is the memory of that one chills me most. We could not get our courage up. Their war cry was the sound of angry seagulls, and we seemed to breathe in death; the look of their faces turned us cold with despair. They struck us aside and went back into the sea, taking Undry with them." He was silent awhile, his light glimmering coldly. "They had broken through the spell-wall. We gave Undry up for lost then, and, binding our power to the three

Treasures we had left, we healed the breach and built up the wall ever higher and stronger. But if they can break through once for Undry, I fear they can again."

Ruth said, her throat dry, "They were Fincara's Women."

"Yes." Ilbrec turned and gazed down at Fand. "I saw her, in the midst of the warriors, and she saw me too, and knew me. Since then, I have never been free from grief."

Ruth looked from him to Fand – the quiet face, the pale hair in the dusk. "But why?" she said at last. "I don't understand. I thought she was your enemy."

Ilbrec was silent. The sun was almost down, the sky fading; and Ilbrec's light was distinct and tangible, like spreading ice. At last Jake put his hand gently on Ruth's shoulder. "Did you not know, Ruthie?" he said quietly. "Ilbrec is Manannan's son. Fand was his mother."

Chapter 13

At last Ilbrec turned back to her. "Well, Fincara's daughter? Will you aid us?"

For a moment Ruth couldn't answer. She felt cold, and the heaviness of Fand's death was in her. Why did Ilbrec ask? Surely everyone could see now how useless she was, how worse than useless. "Me?" she said eventually, her voice coming out dull and reluctant. "What can I do?"

"We need your magic art," said Ilbrec, "to help hold firm the spell-wall. For there is a weakness in it, where it was breached." His golden eyes looked into her, piercing. "One who can break the spell-wall can surely strengthen it again, Fincara's daughter."

"But I can't," said Ruth, her throat dry. "My magic just . . . happens. I can't make it do things. I never even know when it's going to come."

Ilbrec was silent a moment, and Ruth saw his light gather grimly. He said, his voice beginning to resound, "Mortal, Otherworld is not separate from your world; if the dark powers conquer here, the human world too is in danger. Have I not told you this before? And did you not answer, as if prophesying – *It is by humankind that Otherworld will be saved*?"

"Yes," said Ruth huskily. She remembered saying that. She hadn't understood herself then, and didn't now. "But I don't know why I said it."

"Yet you did say it!" His anger broke like a storm, dizzying her. "It is by your magic that we are weakened, and by your magic we may be saved! What cowardice makes you shrink from fulfilling your own prophecy?"

Ruth stood helplessly, able only to let his words batter her. It was true she couldn't control her magic; but, she thought, it's also true I've never tried. And I never will try, because I'm too afraid – too much of a coward to call up that crashing wave and let it kill me. *You'll be always too afraid* . . . She looked away, fixing her eyes on the darkening sea that was visible through the doorway, trying to numb her mind to these unbearable thoughts. Because it *was* unbearable to be such a coward; I'd be better off dead, she thought.

"Peace, Ilbrec!" said Jake quietly. "My friend, you've forgotten what it is to have lived only a short time; you lack patience with us mortals. Leave my daughter be. For remember, it was she who brought my son here, with Undry. But her mother set a cruel spell of fear on her when she was a little child."

"And will Fincara's spells always prevail?" Ilbrec's voice changed, echoingly bleak. "It was an ill day, Jacob, when you married a witch who can turn her own children into our enemies."

"Don't speak so, Ilbrec!" said Jake slowly. Outside the sun was down, and in the dusk he seemed taller, bigger. "I wish only she'd put her spells on me, instead – I'd bear them gladly for my children's sake. And for her sake, too."

He sighed, softly. "For whatever you say of her, Ilbrec, she's my wife; I love her."

Ruth turned, looking at him incredulously. "Ah, Jacob," said Ilbrec, but without anger. "How can you love her still?"

"Some would say, because she gave me a potion to drink from Undry," said Jake. He closed his eyes, as if remembering. "Yet it was before, when I looked from the starr grass and saw her walking out of the sea, when she'd no notion I was even there, that my heart went to her. It was the shine of the sea in her eyes, the dancing look of her, that enraptured me. I drank her drink, but there was no need of it. Since then, she's turned entirely to evil; but she'll never lose my love. It's not possible."

"But Jacob," said Ilbrec, deep-toned, "if you, of all of us, give your heart to an evil witch, how can the powers of light hope to conquer?"

Jake said nothing for a moment, looking quietly at the dim shapes of Sword, Spear and Stone. "It comes to me at times," he said presently, "that our talk of battle and conquering is ignorance. Does not light itself cast shadows? This I hold for a certainty, Ilbrec, that the light and the dark are one thing, of one nature, never to be free of each other. And though we call the creatures of the dark our enemies, and are always in strife with them, yet perhaps there is a greater truth beyond this; and could we but grow in understanding, the light and the dark might be joined, and make a new world beyond all the worlds we know now."

Ilbrec was silent, arms folded; as night came on his form grew ever more distinct, outlined in his own light.

Ruth gazed at her father, aware only that she didn't understand; did Jake mean they should give up the fight? No, she thought; and anyway, how could I give up a fight I've never entered, that I've always been too afraid to join?

Then suddenly Adam began to speak, and her sense of foreboding returned, heavier. Restoring Undry to Andernesse seemed to have brought Adam no relief from Fincara's spell; indeed he looked worse, paler than Fand in the light that washed from the Cauldron. He spoke with a desperate effort, gritting his teeth between phrases, so that he scarcely sounded human.

"Murias was one of the Cities of Light – guarding against the dark. Undry came from there. So Undry must be returned – to let the City rise again – and keep back the dark."

"No!" Ruth cried, and Ilbrec's voice thundered out at the same time, drowning hers in redoubled anger.

"Be silent, boy! You speak as you have been taught, by the witch your mother – you are her creature in everything! If I did not pity your helplessness I would cast you out of here and let you crawl back to her under the sea!"

Ruth was silent, appalled by this harshness. The torture in Adam's face was deepening, but she could see that underneath it all he was still there, desperately holding on to himself through the bewitchment. "No," he said in a whisper. "What I say is *true*."

"Let him speak, Ilbrec," said Jake, low. He stood motionless in the gloom, not looking at his son, as if grief gripped too hard to let him move. "Ah, lad, I should have

150

saved you from this; but I never knew how. Ilbrec, let him speak."

Ruth saw Adam struggling for words, sweat beading his forehead. She'd never before seen him in such conflict, himself against the spell; it brought home to her how powerful Fincara must be. "You call them Treasures," said Adam at last. "You call them precious – powerful. But you shut them in this room – behind a spell-wall – and do *nothing* with them. You let them waste away. Look at them!" He thrust a shaking hand at the worn shapes; they were almost lost now in the night. "Soon they'll just be dust! That – isn't right. Treasures – powers – are for using. To keep back the dark . . . "

He finished, on a long gasp. And Ruth felt something in her go out to his words, in a leap of conviction so strong it shook her; he's right, she thought, not knowing why.

Ilbrec said, his light coldly piercing the dusk, "You speak as she commands you, boy. You're spellbound! You know it yourself! Are we to listen to you?"

Adam closed his eyes briefly. "Jake," he whispered. "Dad – please!"

"No, lad," said Jake grievingly. "Once, perhaps – but you don't understand how long this battle has been, how weakened the powers of light are. We no longer have the wisdom to be sure of using the Treasures rightly."

"Undry was not used rightly, after you lost it," Adam said hoarsely. "And that did you no harm."

"It weakened us. When Undry was lost, the half-mortals bound their power wholly in the three other Treasures – and we daren't risk them, lad! It's a matter now of keeping them safe till we're strong enough to wield them wisely again. Undry too, now that at last we've regained it."

Adam's eyes came, desperately, to Ruth. She stared back at him, full of uncertainty; for surely Jake and Ilbrec must know. And she herself had been sure, before, that Undry belonged in Andernesse ... "It's Fincara making you think that, Adam," she said huskily. "It must be."

"Come," said Ilbrec. "Jacob, bid your son put the Cauldron with the other Treasures. Then we will have them all safe while the spell-wall stands."

Jake turned to Adam, but before he could speak Adam cried, "No!"

Jake gestured with his hands, hopelessly. "Please, lad, please."

"No!" Adam's voice rose in an outrush of despair. He gripped Undry to him, his face twisting in the flow of light. "I've tried! I've listened to you! And all this time she's been calling me to go down into the sea to her – and now I *must* go! Undry must be returned!"

Ruth saw the room whiten with Ilbrec's anger. "Enough! Let Undry be laid in its rightful place!" he thundered, and reached to seize the Cauldron. At that, Ruth saw Adam's face change.

Till then, she'd been able to glimpse him through his bewitchment, and had known he was still there, her brother. But then he seemed to slide from her sight, as if the last of his strength had gone into speaking those words, and now he just gave up. Ruth saw the spell take over completely. His face went smooth and blind, in a kind of collapse; he snatched the Spear from beside Fand, and the worn bronze blade whipped up, levelled.

152

"Keep away from me!"

His voice had changed too, harsh and dead, the sort of voice a devil might have. Ilbrec and Jake froze; Ruth saw Jake's face, rigid with disbelief. Adam backed out through the doorway, still carrying Undry; and, keeping their distance, Ilbrec and Jake followed him on to the hilltop, Ilbrec circling to cut him off from the path. Ruth went too. It was dark enough for stars to show, vague pin-pricks in the black. No one took any notice of her, and she stood helplessly, watching disaster come. I must *do* something, she thought; but her mind felt as empty as the sky, and the thought was lost in it.

Ilbrec said grimly, "Give up the Spear, boy, and the Cauldron – else you will bring death to us all! Can you understand what I say?"

The spear-tip glinted, reflecting Ilbrec's light back at him; for all its age it looked murderously sharp. "I must take Undry to my mother under the sea," Adam said, dull and harsh like a machine.

"No!" Jake cried, pleading. He held both hands out to his son. "Adam," he said, almost as if he were praying, "let this not be!"

"*Let me go*," said Adam. Undry in one hand, the Spear in the other, he stepped towards the path.

"Stop!" Ilbrec thundered, and went for his sword. But Jake moved faster, leaping to snatch the Cauldron away. For a moment Ruth couldn't see what happened in the rush of bodies, the cries, the swirl of light; and then she saw Jake step back with great care, clutching something to his chest – and sink to the ground, the Ildana's Spear standing up weirdly from his ribs. Time seemed to freeze, endlessly. Then Adam, Undry gripped in both hands,

153

thrust past Ilbrec and went running down the path. Ruth listened as the sound of his feet died away into the night.

Silence returned to the hilltop, dense and unreal. Ilbrec went down on his knees by Jake and, gently, drew out the Spear. Ruth saw blood well, sluggishly. Jake was still alive – he looked up at Ilbrec and seemed, strangely, about to smile; then his eyes dulled and turned away, gazing up into the sky.

Ruth said hoarsely, "How badly is he hurt?"

Ilbrec didn't turn to look at her. It was a long time before he answered, and when he did his voice seemed to come coldly out of immense solitudes. "Do not speak to me, girl. Your brother has ended all our hopes now."

Ruth felt ice touch her heart, and spread outwards. And she could only think about herself, not Jake; how she had done nothing, helped no one. *Sensible, reliable, such a help to everyone* . . . but for what really mattered, she was as much use as a block of stone. Even now, it was Ilbrec who knelt gripping Jake's hand – not Jake's daughter.

The half-mortals began to arrive on the hilltop, called in some way Ruth couldn't understand. They carried weapons – swords and spears, helmets and shields – but spoke not a word, their lips grimly set. At last Miach came, kneeling swiftly to examine Jake's wound. Ilbrec rose and stood back to give him room.

To Ruth that felt like the darkest time of the whole night, the stars faint and useless. Even the half-mortals were no more than great still shapes on the hilltop. Miach opened Jake's jacket to bare the wound; hesitated; then fastened it up again, gently.

154

"There is nothing I can do, Ilbrec."

"Nothing, healer?" Ilbrec's voice echoed round the hilltop. "For shame!"

"I cannot call back the dying." Miach rose, and stood as if in thought. "That is not my art. Sickness I can cure, pain I can ease, but over the departing soul I have no power. Ilbrec, none struck by the Ildana's Spear can hope to live."

Ilbrec was silent. Watching, Ruth remembered she'd never thought him young, like Miach; but his face seemed withered now, age coming on him like winter. Presently he lifted his hands and spoke, but the words were beyond ordinary language; Ruth felt as if stars came down to earth and stood around him, mourning. She had to hide her face in her hands. She'd loved Jake herself, but not like this.

At last Kilgrimol grew still again, and she looked up. Ilbrec turned towards her, his light raying coldly round him. "Go from here, Fincara's child; for I cannot bear to set eyes on you, after what your brother has done. I should have cast you both out of Andernesse long ago. Now it is too late; go, and use your magic to save yourself from what is coming."

Ruth's throat tightened. "What do you mean?" she said after a moment. "What's going to happen?"

"The dark is entering Andernesse. Our power is at an end, for your brother used the Ildana's Spear to murder his father." Ilbrec regarded her, shedding a cold changeless light. "The spell-wall is down. We cannot raise it again. The hosts of darkness are swarming in on Andernesse. We shall remain here, and hold Kilgrimol to the last – but Andernesse is lost, Fincara's daughter, lost to your mother's evil magic and the treachery of her children."

Ruth looked down towards the sea. The spell-wall had vanished – melted like a dream. And she could see an army marshalling on the shore, unfurling black banners; she saw pale faces, and silver helmets. Fincara had sent her Women into the last great battle. A war cry lifted into the night, cold and piercing like a gull's scream.

Ilbrec said, "Go now, and save yourself!"

Ruth looked across at where Jake lay. He was still just alive; she saw his eyes move, slowly scanning the sky. But it wouldn't be long now – soon he would be dead, like Fand. It was as if all her own life were draining away, losing all it had held to. The only person left was mad Adam.

She turned and followed him down the path.

Chapter 14

Down in the Forest it was so dark that she had to walk with her hands stretched out, stumbling and knocking into trees. But gradually a fierce pale shimmer grew, intensifying to a glare that she recognized; and the seagull screeching became more distinct. She halted, pressing herself to the trunk of an oak. And then Fincara's Women were sweeping past, helmets flashing, spears icily burning; if they saw her they took no notice, going by like freezing waves. There seemed to be thousands of them, all making for Kilgrimol. It was a long time before the last had passed.

Ruth moved from the shelter of the oak tree then, and went on. She had no idea where she was going, but she kept on steadily. It would be easier, she thought, just to sit down and wait for the Women to find me, or for the powers of light to be completely overcome ... Neither idea frightened her, which was strange; she couldn't understand herself. She'd heard of people with fearsome wounds who felt no pain at all at first, who calmly walked miles before collapsing; this must be what it's like, she thought. But presently there was a salt tang on the night breeze, and she knew then where she was heading. The trees parted, and she stepped out on to the beach.

It was easier to see; the tide was full in, faintly casting back the starlight. The sand was a dim paleness, deeply trampled by the army that had landed. Ruth stood, looking. At the edge of the water Adam knelt, Undry in his hands.

"Adam," she said. Her voice sounded distant, different, as if it belonged to someone else. Adam looked out to sea, his face so deep in enchantment that she knew there was no point reminding him what he'd done.

More strangely, she didn't want to. What good would it do? Fand was dead, Jake dying, all the half-mortals about to die – she felt frozen by these immensities. I ought to be dead too, she thought.

She went over to Adam and knelt by him, reaching to touch his cold hands. "What are we going to do, Adam?" she asked.

He turned his face to her. "I must take Undry to Caer Wydyr."

"But it doesn't matter any more," Ruth said. "The powers of the dark have won now. Fincara doesn't need Undry."

"Yes, she does – to make her great amongst the dark powers. She's calling me to go. And I'd have to go anyway; it's what I'm for."

Ruth was silent. The Women's voices had risen distantly to a shriek, and she could hear hammering clashes of sound – spear against shield, sword against helmet. So that was how a battle sounded. She could hear the half-mortals too, answering – their voices were deeper than the Women's, tolling like great bells. She wondered how long it would take them to be defeated.

"Shall I come with you, Adam?" she said, and listened to her words with the faintest sense of surprise. I'm not frightened any more, she thought; I'm not anything; there's nothing in me but emptiness. Perhaps I've already started to die.

"You have to come," said Adam. "She's calling you too. That's why you're here on the shore."

Ruth wondered if that were true. Perhaps it explained why she'd come straight here, without hesitating; and looking inside herself she could discern a faint tugging, an urging to wade out into the sea. Fincara must want to finish me off, make quite sure I'm no threat to her, she thought. But the calling seemed weak; she could have ignored it easily.

Adam rose to his feet. "Ruth: we must go."

Ruth got up slowly. I don't have to, she thought. I could wait here, alone, for everything to end. But...

But she'd let down too many people – Fand, Jake, Ilbrec. Adam was the only one left. She looked at him, pale in the starlight, his face tightening as Fincara called him ever more insistently from the depths of the sea. I can't leave him, she thought. I can't do anything to save him, but I can at least go with him back to Caer Wydyr. It's not as if I'm afraid any more. How like me, to stop being afraid only when everything's lost...

She reached out and took his hand. "Come on, then."

They waded out into the water. Still warm from the day, it lapped silkily round their legs; and Ruth felt Fincara's magic stretch out for them. There was a moment when she could still feel the hard ribbed sand under her feet;

then it was gone, and they were slipping under.

It was strange, that weightless plunge into the depths. Ruth glimpsed a porpoise diving, then a school of flickering silver fish; then they were down in the blackness where no light reached. We've no Sea People's cloaks this time, Ruth thought; only Fincara's magic can keep us from drowning. Somehow she knew she wouldn't drown. Yet the magic felt curiously flimsy, not at all like the great force that had swept her away at other times. This seemed only to work because neither she nor Adam resisted.

Adam gasped, "Look!"

Ruth saw Undersea spread tinily below. It was a bigger country than she'd expected – shadowy hills, lakes and plains, beneath the mysterious silvery-green drift. There was even a city, domes and spires glimmering like reflections in water. Ruth felt an instant's wrench at the thought that the powers of darkness would soon take it all over completely; but what's the good of grieving? she thought. What can I do? I'll soon be dead, anyway; Fincara will see to that . . . She saw the emerald-coloured river, flowing down to the Drowned Forest. And the island.

"Caer Wydyr!" Adam cried.

And suddenly they were there, in the separate world of the Glass Castle. It was as Ruth remembered; the Great Tower stood before them, seamed with fire. Stiffening in the cold, she watched the white flames spit and rage in blackness. After everything, she had ended up back here; and it felt like the end, for surely no one could escape twice from Caer Wydyr.

"What good children, to come so quick at my calling!"

160

Fincara was there, long hair tossing in the light, her face afire with laughter. It's now, Ruth thought; we'll die now, go down in the blaze of the Castle with Fincara laughing. It hardly seemed to matter. She still had hold of Adam's hand, and tightened her grip childishly.

Fincara's eyes met hers, seeming to hold a measuring look behind the laughter. "Well, daughter? Did it work, the spell I laid on you never to use your power? Except for dragging your brother from here in such panic, have you worked any magic?"

Ruth swallowed. "Once, to go to Andernesse. But never meaning to. I was always too afraid."

Fincara threw back her head and laughed – a pitch of mirth that but for its mockery might have sounded like relief. "Your trip to Andernesse served my turn, child, letting Adam stick that Spear in his fool of a father! I myself could not have done better!"

That's true, Ruth thought; that's true. And though she'd believed all her pain was over, at that some bitter pangs returned.

Taking no more notice of her, Fincara turned to Adam and stretched out her hands, quick and arrogant. "Give me the Cauldron, boy!"

Adam was silent, not moving; and Fincara's eyes widened, sharply, as if only now truly seeing him. Ruth saw that shadows seemed to cluster round Undry; and suddenly Adam pulled out of her grip to hold it in both hands, tightly. The tortured look had returned to his face. "No . . . " It was a long gasp. "I must hang Undry from the golden chains myself!"

"What?" Fincara stepped towards him, her voice

161

suddenly jagged as broken glass. "All you must do is my bidding, boy; you've brought Undry here as I told you, so now give it me!"

"No . . . " Adam hugged Undry blindly. "*Don't*, mother! Can't you see? You made me the one to bring Undry back, and I must bring it *right* back – to its own place in Murias!"

Ruth felt herself tensing. She hadn't expected this; she'd thought only of an easy surrender, a sliding down into darkness. Surely Fincara could let Adam hang Undry from the chains, if he wanted to; what did it matter? But she saw that, to Fincara, it did matter.

"*Give me Undry!*" Her hands were claws, her voice a gull's shriek. "None but I shall hang it from the chains; it shall do my bidding, no other's! Loose it, boy – I command you!" The power crackled from her, the whole Castle flaming.

Ruth saw that force of magic break round Adam. He lifted his face to it, Undry clasped to his chest – and all the old craziness descended, ten times worse. Undry and Fincara tore him in two, and he could obey neither of them. Ruth stared; she'd never thought this would happen; and she knew, suddenly, that she couldn't let it.

It was as if, in the emptiness inside her, someone stood up and spoke. The words were echoingly clear: *Ruth Demdyke, you have let Fand die and your brother suffer madness; you have let your father be killed, and the half-mortals go into a battle they cannot win. Yet with your power you could have prevented all this. Now at last you have come to the end of your fear; you have one chance left. Fight!*

162

She felt strange to herself, as if she were suddenly far away; she could still see Caer Wydyr, but it seemed small and distant. She raised her hand and saw she held a great spear like a shaft of pure light, silvery-gold, with intertwined engraving that moved as if alive. "Fincara!" she said, and her voice sounded strange too, ringing and reverberating. "I challenge you!"

Fincara turned, unbelievingly: and Ruth saw her face change, eyes going as dead as stones. "*No!*" she screamed, reaching out; and a black spear sprang into each hand. "*I'll not be stopped by my daughter's magic!*"

My mother, Ruth thought with an unfamiliar pang; but then there was no room for thoughts.

It was hard afterwards to remember what happened. She knew they were no longer in Caer Wydyr; they'd come to a place outside time, winds of space roaring round them. She was conscious only of the blinding spear, and a fear that it might destroy the whole world if she wasn't careful; it was too huge, too strong. She saw Fincara hurl her black spears, one after the other, but they were little and frail, and broke up before they even reached her; and Fincara's changed face was before her, screaming. Then she launched her spear. And as the power stormed through her she knew she'd been right to fear her magic; it was like all the seas of all the worlds in the day of their destruction.

Only Adam saw. On his knees, the rim of Undry pressing into his chest, he'd been conscious of their voices, though too far gone to understand what they said; he was caught in Fincara's magic, a fly in a web, mind and will

163

spreadeagled hopelessly. But then he looked up and saw two figures as tall as the sky, outlined in fire, great spear-blades whipping like lightning. It was only a glimpse; even to Adam's deeply enchanted eyes, they were not really visible. He fell, sprawling face down on the icy glass, both hands still gripping Undry. When he began to be able to think, he thought he'd been struck blind.

But he hadn't. Presently he began to hear only the hiss of white fire which, in the Castle, was like the sound of silence. He could move; and though he felt numbed, stricken, utterly mad, he could collect his wits after a fashion. He sat up, clasping Undry.

It was Fincara he saw first. She lay as he had done, face down, her hair spread out smooth like glinting silk. For one so powerful she looked little and frail, a broken doll. Standing beside her, Ruth looked hardly any stronger – head hanging, shoulders slumped. Then she looked up, and he flinched; she'd changed beyond recognition, her face a stranger's, *old* – though still a girl, older somehow than anyone he could think of. Then she looked at him and gradually a shadow of the Ruth he knew crept back.

She said in a whisper, "Go and return Undry to its place, Adam."

He could get up. There was no more magic turning his limbs to stone and stripping his soul from his body. He could move; he didn't even slip on the glass. But Undry had grown, needing two hands now to carry it – white as silver, he saw, with pearls glowing round the rim, and light spilling over his fingers. He could do now what it needed of him. He began to walk over the cracked glass, between the flashing ruins, towards the Great Tower.

Ruth watched him. Her body felt cramped and cold, like something she'd just returned to. *Consumed like tinder*, she thought, *emptied out like water* ... she hadn't understood Miach's words till now. Her magic had also – she glanced at Fincara's prone form – conquered her mother. *I believed she was so powerful*, Ruth thought dully, *after what she did to Adam – after what she did to me, too; but in fact her power was nothing to mine.* And she felt no triumph for that, only a sorrow she couldn't master, a distress without end.

She saw Adam enter the Great Tower. Undry had begun to shine, like a milky opal clearing to reveal its fires; and now she could see it glowing through the splintered walls of the Tower. Adam lifted it, reaching for the chains. He hooked one chain to Undry's rim; then another chain. Strangely, Ruth's heart lifted. Adam hooked on the third chain.

She hadn't known what to expect; but it wasn't this. Undry's glow leapt outward, filling all the Castle, and in that instant the broken towers stood up whole. Then the floor thrust against her feet, and she saw green water curl away above; they were shooting up through the sea. But she saw no more. She'd held on too long, and there was a quiet blackness reaching out for her, more and more commandingly. *I can't do any more*, she thought; *I'm finished.* She was conscious of great winds of light circling round about, but they were no longer anything to do with her; *I'm going*, she thought very clearly, and at once felt herself slip down and down into the cradling dark.

Chapter 15

Gradually she woke up. She'd only ever fainted once before, but she remembered the sensation of extreme weakness, muscles papery and helpless. She lay still, remembering also that the weakness soon went, and then you felt much better than before; which presently happened, allowing her to sit, and look round – and then, amazed, to stand.

She was on the outermost parapet of a Castle, looking up at its towers. The Castle was made, she thought, of neither glass nor crystal, but purest light; it seemed to float like a cloud, ready at any moment to melt and re-form. Yet it was no mirage, but solid under her feet. And the light didn't dazzle, washing her like clearest springwater.

Beside her, steps went down to a courtyard planted with trees and flowers. It seemed to be spring, she thought, looking down; it had been summer in both Andernesse and Wickrithe, but here daffodils and primroses edged the paths, and there were mists of bluebells, and hawthorns white with may blossom. Even the flowers seemed like tiny suns, delicately glowing. She wanted to go down, but something – some awe – held her back.

She turned to look at the island on which the Castle stood. It was the only land in sight under the blue sweep of sky; the ocean, a darker blue, rolled limitlessly to the horizon. Until now it hadn't occurred to her to wonder who she was and where she came from; but the little green isle, with the high rock on which the Castle stood, and a stream winding between willow trees to a white beach, woke her memory. "I'm Ruth Demdyke," she thought – and at that remembered everything.

The pain was bewildering. Because I'm not used to it, she thought, dazed; I've always been able to hide before from things I didn't like. But now . . . all her defences were gone, and the remorse wrung her like a rag. She'd been a coward. She'd let everyone down. Otherworld had fallen to the dark powers and she hadn't lifted a finger. Only right at the end had she stood up and fought – and then it had been against her own mother. She leant her arms on the parapet and hid her face in them, wishing she hadn't woken from her faint.

"Do not weep." The voice was like silver ringing, and very close to her. "Welcome, oh welcome, Spell-breaker, to Murias!"

Ruth looked up, startled. A slender woman stood before her, dressed in a gown the colour of rippling sea-water; her hair was long and fair, her eyes bright as tears but full of peace. *Murias*, Ruth thought . . .

"Do you not know me?" The woman began to smile. "Come, mortal, remember! I am Fand!"

Ruth stared, and for a moment couldn't speak. For this was quite impossible. But she saw the face like ivory, the long floating hair, and felt the sense of freedom spreading from her . . . "Fand," she said, and it all came back with redoubled force – the betrayal, the guilt. "But – you died . . ."

Fand took her by the hands, and her touch was warm, living. And her voice when she spoke was as strong as the light, full of solace and certainty. "When you say that I died, you mean only that I shall be seen no more in your world. Yet even there I shall come from time to time, and may be seen by those who have the eyes for it. But, dearest of my friends, this is Murias. Here there are few things which are not possible."

"I don't understand," said Ruth with difficulty. "I just don't see how you can ever forgive me."

"Ruth!" whispered Fand – laughing, though in her laughter there was something more solemn than silence. "Have you not realized? We stand here in Murias – Murias raised from the sea, to guard the world once more against the dark! And it is your doing – you conquered the Witch, broke her enchantments, and let your brother hang Undry once more from its golden chains. Look – only look!"

Ruth looked. Taking her hand, Fand led her down the steps into the courtyard, and they stood amongst the bluebells, surrounded by the soaring towers. Ruth looked up, feeling as if she breathed in light – feeling that just to stand there was a greater adventure than anything that had ever happened to her. Haltingly, she said, "But they told us Andernesse was the only safe place for Undry. They said if we took it back to Caer Wydyr, darkness would win."

"But see!" Fand whispered.

Ruth saw. Every time she looked, the towers seemed taller, veiling the whole sky in light. And as she looked

168

and looked, it seemed all her fear, guilt and self-contempt blew away like dust, leaving her nothing but wonder. "Adam knew," she said at last. "But we didn't listen to him. We just thought he was bewitched."

"Do not reproach yourself," said Fand. "In the world of mortals it is hard, very hard, to be wise. Yet you should never fear; it is the way of mortals to find in their deepest despair their highest victory. For see how you have conquered!"

"But I was such a coward," said Ruth. "I never did anything – just kept hoping it would all somehow stop. I only challenged Fincara because I thought the powers of darkness had won, and nothing worse could happen to me."

"Ah, Ruth," said Fand softly, "inside us all is a battle between dark and light – between fear and the power in us to do good. Some give in to the fear and spend all their lives in the dark, never knowing what they could have done; and indeed it is a hard battle to fight. But even the fear can be a guide, pointing to where our true powers lie; and so it was with you, Ruth. For now you know you possess a magic so great that all the worlds depend on you – so great, it must never again be denied."

Ruth was silent, conscious of ideas almost too huge for her mind to grasp. For it was her cowardice, her running away, that had led her step by step to that place outside time where she had faced Fincara, spear-edge to spear-edge. It was beyond understanding, how fear had led to the thing most feared, and beyond that to freedom from all fear. She touched the creamy blossoms of hawthorn, inhaling their sweet, piercing scent.

"But it was my own mother," she said, low. "I know I

didn't love her; and she didn't love me; she only tried to bewitch me; but ... "

"Yes." Fand looked at her sadly. "Often in the battle we must turn our power against those nearest to us. Has my son not told you how once I bore weapons against him? And though I understand now that Undry had to be taken from Andernesse before it could be restored in Murias ... even so, the grief of that night still lives in me."

Ruth looked at the brightness of her eyes. "Oh, Fand," she said.

"No, do not pity me; for I am freed of my deepest griefs now. Freed too are my sisters; and so is your brother, for he has accomplished his task and need bear no more burdens. Andernesse is saved, for in ancient days it lay under the protection of Murias; and the half-mortals are safe. As for Fincara" – Fand smiled, still with that faint sadness – "you worked your magic well, Ruth, for not a hair of her head is harmed, though after your battle all her power is gone."

Ruth closed her eyes briefly; she couldn't quite understand the relief that came. She would never, she thought, fully comprehend her tangled feelings for her mother. Whereas for Jake ...

"Fand," she said slowly, "did Jake – really die?"

Fand smiled. "He is safe. Do not fear for him, Ruth. For though his wound is deadly, the water of Undry can heal him, now Murias is once more raised. Come. It is time for you to see Undry."

She led Ruth to a doorway, and through it into another courtyard. This was bigger than the first, with long glimmering lawns full of daisies, and buttercups just beginning to show. There was an oak tree in one corner, and Ruth could hear a blackbird singing. But in the centre stood a great round tower, shedding such a glory of light that Ruth had to stop, feeling her breath come and go as if she were in a race. By moments it was as if tall figures moved there, and sometimes great crowds, many turning to smile at her; yet when she looked she could see nothing but the tower, the lawns and the oak tree.

"Fand," she said at last, breathlessly, "it feels as if there's more here than just what you can see."

"So there is," said Fand gently. "It is said that in the Castle of Murias lies a City, in the City a Realm, in the Realm a World, and in that World, all the Worlds. Though I am but new to Murias, I know this to be true. But do not fear, Ruth; I shall not take you beyond the Castle. Yet you would have a dull spirit if you could not feel here the turning of the Worlds."

"It's the light, too," said Ruth. She looked up at the tower, feeling she hardly *saw* any more; her eyes, all her senses, were too limited for this. "I think it's too much for me."

"It is Murias. Here light reigns without any shadows; even the undying are sometimes dazzled. But you can bear it for a little while."

Ruth followed her towards the Tower; indeed, she couldn't have borne not to, though she thought this light might well be the death of her. She seemed to be moving beyond herself; she felt hardly in her body any more as she stepped over the threshold.

And there was Undry, a great perfect pearl hanging

171

from the golden chains, full to the brim with – not water, Ruth thought, but liquid jewels. Light rose from it as dense as smoke. Dazzled, she looked down at the intertwined engraving, and saw it no longer seemed unfinished; the curved, sweeping lines completed themselves, like words of peace written in the language of light.

She couldn't have said how long she stood there, gazing, breathing in the light. She guessed later that there was no time in that Tower, only the sense of a perfect homecoming, a joy like arms around her. It's as if it's a place I've always known, she thought, as if I remember it; but how could I? How could I even have imagined a place like this?

Presently a dark-haired boy came towards her, saying, "Ruth."

She gazed at him. She supposed no one in the Tower could ever look quite like themselves, but he seemed . . . transfigured: so truly alive that she wondered how she recognized him. "Adam," she said. "You're changed."

He shook his hair back, lifting his face to the light and smiling. I haven't seen him smile before, Ruth thought; not really *smile* . . .

"I never knew what it was like, not to be bewitched," he said. Even his voice had changed – deeper, fuller, as if he had suddenly learnt to breathe more easily. He looked at her, thoughtful and wondering. "It's so queer, Ruth. Like – I don't know."

"Like coming out of prison," Ruth said. "That's what you look like."

He smiled again, the thoughtfulness lingering in his

172

eyes. "Yes. But more than that. I always used to feel – empty inside, as if I wasn't really anyone. Then Fincara brought her spell back into my mind, and that filled me, so that I couldn't be anyone even if I tried. And I did try, at times ... "

"Yes," said Ruth. "I know."

"I thought, once the spell went, I'd be empty again. I was *afraid* of it going. But now it has, and ... "

"And you're someone," said Ruth. She looked into his face; as with Fand, the sense of freedom spread from him like rays. "I can see. The fears are all gone and you know now what your true powers are."

"Something like that." He looked at her consideringly. "You're changed, too. You're not afraid any more."

"How could I be, here?"

"No." Adam gazed round, his face full of light. "It's like coming home. Why do I feel as if I've been here before – as if I've always been waiting to come back?"

"I don't know. I do too."

They stood, watching Undry. It's as if the Adam I knew before was just the shadow, Ruth thought, and now he's real. That shows how Fincara's spells crippled him ... Looking, she could see there was still a darkness at the back of his eyes, a memory of what he had been – a memory, she guessed, that he would never quite lose.

Presently Fand came forward, taking from the folds of her gown a tiny phial of clear glass. She held it out to Adam. "Mortal," she said gravely, "in Andernesse there lies one sorely hurt at your hands. Take this, and fill it with the waters of Undry, that you may return and heal him."

173

Adam took the phial, his brow knitting; and Ruth saw the shadows return to his face. After a moment he said, rather desperately, "I never meant to hurt him!"

Sadness touched Fand again, a look like tears shining. "Ah, mortal," she said, almost in a whisper, "I too have been under spells; and for many of the deeds I did bewitched, I weep. Still, here, in Murias, I weep."

Adam stood silent, gripping the phial. Then he said, with difficulty, "If Jake's – dead – will it still work?"

"Yes," said Fand gently. "Therefore you may take only a little. For it is a forbidden thing, to bring the dead back to life."

"Forbidden?" Adam repeated.

"Yes. But this once, not to you, mortal. For you and your sister have been very valiant. Come, fill the phial."

Adam turned to fill the tiny bottle and fasten the stopper in, tightly. Full of Undry's water, it shone in his fingers. He turned back to Fand. "Can we go now?" he said, low.

"Yes." Fand smiled, her eyes glimmering very bright. "Bid each other farewell."

Ruth felt herself gasp. "Farewell?" she repeated. "But—"

Adam looked at her. And Ruth felt she hadn't seen till now the depth of change in him; he seemed to have grown taller than her since touching Undry's water, and his face was a man's, not a boy's. But he's younger than me, Ruth thought; he's *only fourteen* . . . But the light clouded across, and she knew people had no ages in Murias. He looks like Jake, she thought: a man. He

174

regarded her, steady and sure, as if his inward gaze was set on some horizon that only he knew of. Before he even spoke, Ruth felt deeply alone.

"Ruth," he said, "I'm not coming back to Wickrithe. I can't. What could I do there?"

He couldn't, she saw that. He'd never belonged there; trapped from his birth in Fincara's magic, he'd never been able to grow into the ordinary world. Otherworld was where he belonged; like Jake. "Where will you go, then?" she asked huskily.

"To Kilgrimol, first, to heal Jake. And then . . ." She could see his eyes move to that long horizon. "If they'll let me, I'll take the Spear of the Ildana and go back to Gorias with it."

Ruth was silent, words impossible. Nothing ever happens as you expect, she thought; I believed we'd come to the end of all the dangers. And now, too, we'll never see each other again . . . It was strange, since she hardly knew this changed Adam, since he was all but a stranger, to feel such a piercing sense of loss. She looked away. "What about me, Fand?" she said, feeling desolate with the newness of it all. "I don't want to go. I want to stay here . . ."

"No, Ruth." Fand came forward to face her across Undry, with a hint of sadness. "Though your power is very great, it is not time yet for you to make your home in Murias. You must go back to your own world. There is much to do there, and you will be needed."

"Can't I come back?" said Ruth. "Won't I ever see you again?"

Fand smiled. "Never doubt that! Our souls hold each

175

other fast. Why, Murias was destroyed and lost till you raised it again; and shall you be shut out from it? Ruth, there will be a time when we shall walk together through every pathway of Murias, and learn to know each court and tower; and none shall send you away. For you shall know everything then."

Ruth could find no answer; for Undry's light seemed to fill her, leaving no room for speech. Was this grief, or joy? She couldn't tell; it seemed beyond either of them.

Fand reached out, taking each of them by the hand for a moment. "Farewell, mortals," she said softly. "But before you go, drink from Undry. For you have earned this right."

They both stooped to drink, the glory all round their faces. Ruth cupped her hands and scooped up the jewel-like water.

The taste was fresh as spring, sharp as wine. It seemed to sweep her into a new world, truer and more real than the worlds she'd known before; a place of endless radiance, where the voice of Undry spoke, telling of perfect peace. For an instant she was merged entirely in the light, not existing apart from it; and what she still knew of fear and sorrow all fell away from her. Yes, she thought, her mind utterly clear: yes, I understand now. And as she felt herself returning to the shadowy shores of her own world, she knew she carried that understanding with her: a sure secret, that only Undry could bestow.

Chapter 16

Ruth went through the empty guest house, checking to see nothing was left behind. She could hear them talking outside, Aunt Sarah helping Gran into the car, Jenny fetching the rug for her legs, Uncle Nick and Robin loading the cases. Already the house felt shut up and abandoned, the dank smell of the flood mounting from the basement.

No one had actually asked what had happened to her. She'd returned into a cold dawn to find that the flood-waters were going down, and that she'd lost only about ten hours of this world's time. Gran and the guests had been up all night, watching helplessly as the water poured into the house and flooded the basement; in that chaos, the fact of her safe return was enough, and the only questions asked were about Adam. "I saw him last on Starr Hills," Ruth said eventually and, seeing the look of loss in her face, Gran and the guests knew Adam had been drowned.

Of course the police had to be told, and Ruth wondered if she was in some state of shock, for she felt quite numb as she lied her way through an interview with a sympathetic young constable: yes, she'd seen Adam go on to

Starr Hills; no, she hadn't followed him. Plainly believing her, the young man said gently, "I'm sorry, but if he was on the Hills when the flood broke through, he won't have had a chance. I doubt we'll even find the body; knowing the currents round there, he'll have been carried right out to sea when the water went down. We'll look, of course." And at that, unreasoningly, pain harrowed Ruth; she sat with tears pouring down her face, feeling more a liar than ever – for she knew better than anyone that there was no need to cry for Adam. She looked across to where Gran sat, as still as stone, and felt as if she were crying for the whole world.

All the guests left that same day. Ruth put Gran to bed in one of the upstairs rooms, and coped with the fire brigade when they arrived to pump out the basement. It wasn't water so much as liquid mud; everything down there was ruined and the smell wouldn't go. Then the social services came with paraffin heaters and a camping stove, but however Ruth tried she couldn't seem to get Gran warm again. She was thankful when Aunt Sarah and Uncle Nick arrived with Jenny and Robin, having seen the flood on breakfast television.

They took one look at Gran and decided not to try moving her that day. "Tomorrow, Ma," Uncle Nick said, giving her one of his gentlest bear hugs. "Tomorrow we're taking you to Coniston and you can put your feet up for as long as you like. What do you say?" Gran smiled faintly but said nothing.

The rest of the day was one long rush – sending for the doctor for Gran, going to the Town Hall to ask about compensation for flood damage, seeing what could be salvaged from the ground floor. Ruth fetched and carried, doing what she was told, but she felt half invisible; no one knew what had happened to her, no one even guessed there was anything to know. While she was packing a suitcase for Gran, she whispered to herself, "Murias has been saved"; but it sounded like another language.

Even Aunt Sarah didn't seem to notice anything different about her. Ruth knew she ought not to expect it, while Gran lay there so cold and quiet, like marble. Perhaps Aunt Sarah did notice something, but just ascribed it to the flood, and Adam's death. The doctor came, and couldn't talk about anything but the flood either. None of them can see past what happens in this world, Ruth thought; perhaps there won't ever be anyone I can tell.

They all found beds for the night in the upstairs rooms. But Ruth couldn't sleep, even though she felt she'd been awake for about a week now; it was too cold for summer, and the dank, strong, seaweedy smell from the basement seemed to come between her and sleep. And Gran was on her conscience; I can't let her go on thinking Adam's dead, she thought. But how can I tell her? She'll think I'm crazy.

But at last it became too miserable, lying there shivering and thinking round in circles. Ruth got up, so tired that she felt disembodied, almost floating. She pulled on a sweater and found her way to Gran's room.

Gran was awake. Ruth could see the little blue flame of

179

the paraffin heater reflected in her eyes. She sat on the side of the bed and felt for the knuckly old hand. It was as cold as glass.

"Gran. About Adam. He isn't drowned."

Gran never moved. But Ruth felt the old eyes watching her through the darkness.

She said, "He's with Jake. They won't ever come back now. They're in . . . Otherworld." She hesitated, doubting; but when she'd almost decided not to say any more, she felt Gran press her hand, just perceptibly.

"Go on, lass." It was the faintest of whispers.

So Ruth told her everything. Crouched there on the side of the bed, warming her free hand over the paraffin heater when she got too cold, Ruth told her about Undry and the land Undersea, Caer Wydyr and Andernesse, Adam, Jake, Fincara and the Ildana's Spear. And Gran lay there motionless, listening. Ruth told it right through to the end, dwelling on the crystal towers of Murias.

"Now what on earth!" said Aunt Sarah, opening the door. "You need your sleep, Ruth love, and your Gran certainly does."

"Don't you scold her," said Gran with unexpected vigour, making them both start. "She's done me good. I shan't die now."

"Ma, for heaven's sake don't talk like that," said Aunt Sarah, taken aback. "Here's another hot-water bottle for you. Of course you're not going to die."

"I'd near made up my mind to," said Gran, accepting the hot-water bottle.

"Well, just unmake it again. I do wish you wouldn't say

these things, Ma. You'll upset people."

"What people, I should like to know?"

"Me," said Aunt Sarah, tucking her up. "You'll upset me."

"Nowt wrong wi' that," said Gran with the ghost of a smile, shutting her eyes. "You've upset me enough in your time, you and Jake between you."

Aunt Sarah laughed and hugged her. But Ruth stared; it was the first time she'd heard Gran speak Jake's name so lightly. The old face looked peaceful, as if a weight had been lifted. Ruth went back to bed, finding Aunt Sarah had left her a hot-water bottle as well, and curled up with it thankfully. Had Gran understood her, then, and believed her? That was like a weight lifting, too.

But, as she checked round the empty house next day before they left for Coniston, the loneliness came back doubly hard. She couldn't understand herself. When I was in Otherworld, she thought, I was terrified nearly all the time; but now all I want is to be back there. Why couldn't I have stayed, like Adam and Jake and Fincara? Why was I the only one to be sent home again? It isn't home any more . . . She looked out of the window at the garden and the back lane, almost clear now of river mud, and the view was as alien as if she'd never seen it before. She stood there so long, grappling with her feelings, that Uncle Nick grew impatient and honked the car horn for her.

She took no notice. This must be how Jake used to feel, she thought; once you've been in Otherworld half of you

181

stays there, and you can't belong in this world again. People don't know, don't understand; no one can, who hasn't been there too. They just think you're queer – standing staring out of a window when everyone else is ready to go ... *What's the matter with Ruth? It's not like her to hold us up.* Only Gran would know why, and she would sit there not saying anything.

At that moment Otherworld seemed so lost and irrecoverable that Ruth really wondered if it had just been a dream. Perhaps it was, she thought; perhaps I just imagined it all. I've been under stress this summer ... Maybe Jake was only a halfwit, Fincara just a spoilt woman who left him, and Undry itself no more than a battered old cup. And Adam ... Adam was just a crazy boy who drowned in the flood. Ruth stood there, staring out of the window, her heart so heavy she could hardly bear it.

"Ruthie."

She jerked round, startled. She hadn't heard anyone come up. He stood there, looking hesitant and ill, a surgical dressing taped on his brow.

"Ben!" She remembered the night of the flood, Adam hitting him, and guilt stabbed her. "Are you all right?"

"Aye." He smiled. "I've a thick head. The water woke me up when it started coming in fast, and the hospital's nobbut a step down the road."

"I'm sorry," said Ruth. "Adam ... " She didn't know how to go on.

He took a step into the room, awkwardly. "I've come at

a bad time, love. Your uncle says I'm to send you down; he's in a hurry to be gone. But . . . " he hesitated. "There's a thing I wanted to tell you, Ruthie."

Ruth was already looking up at him, but at that she felt her face change – with a desperate sort of hope, perhaps. It seemed to give Ben confidence.

"When I was sitting there in the hospital, waiting for me head to be stitched, I seemed to go into a sort of dream, love. I saw, clear as anything, a green hill with a little thatched house on it, and the sun rising. Your brother was there."

Ruth felt herself gasp. "Was Jake there?" she said. "Ben, was Jake there too?"

"Aye. With a look to him – eh, I can hardly tell you – as if he'd come back from somewhere so far, he could barely remember himself. Yet he was smiling, and holding your brother by the shoulders, like he'd been given summat he'd stopped hoping for." Ben sighed, remembering. "And your brother – he had a spear in his hands, and I heard him say – 'Come with me, and we'll take it to Gorias, and bring the gold towers back.' "

Ruth caught her breath, the words seeming to clash in her ears like sudden trumpets. Kilgrimol was vivid in her mind, the distant mountains fiery with dawn, the trees alive in the morning wind.

She said, after what felt like a long silence, "Was it a little bronze spear, very worn?"

"Eh, no, love. A great flashing thing like gold, wi' red and blue enamel shining in the blade."

Ruth was silent; then nodded.

183

"Then," said Ben, "they turned to the sky, and Jake pointed. There was the sun coming up, and the clouds all afire; and for a minute, it was like gold towers there in the east of the sky. Plain as plain. And they set off down the hill with the sun in their faces, all three of them."

"Three?"

"Aye." Ben looked at her gently. "Your mother was there too."

"*Fincara?*"

"Aye. But not how I remembered her." Ben paused, thinking. "She used to be the loveliest woman I've ever seen – but shivery, if you take my meaning. She put a chill in you. I used always to be tongue-tied in front of her, feeling a right fool; I was afraid of her, Ruthie, if you want the truth. But now she looked ... more ordinary, like. And not just because her hair's started to go grey, and her looks aren't the same – though that's true. She looked as if a human soul had come back into her. She was clinging to Jake's arm, and there were tears in her eyes; and the way she looked up at him ... she always used to laugh at him, love; but she wasn't laughing now. And he held her to him, tender, like a child. You know?"

"Yes," said Ruth. She could feel the tears coming to her own eyes. Oh, Jake ... "Yes, I know."

"It all faded, then," said Ben. "And a nurse called me in to the doctor."

Ruth was silent, her mind a whirl. She remembered these feelings from when she'd stood by Undry in Murias, an impossible mixture of joy and pain. So it was real, she thought; it was all real.

Ben said with a hint of sadness, "I thought, I'll come and tell Ruthie. Happen she'll know what it all means. But now you're off to Coniston, aren't you? Eh, love, I'm going to miss you and your Gran."

Ruth could feel a warmth expanding inside her. Joy was winning out over the pain. Looking out of the window, she saw the clouds had broken, revealing a patch of blue. She turned back to Ben, and smiled at him. "It's all right," she said. "We're only going for Gran to have a rest, and get over the shock. She'll be OK. And then we'll be back."

He looked at her doubtfully. "What – you as well, Ruthie?"

"Yes," said Ruth. She didn't know when she'd come to that decision, but she found, to her surprise, it was quite settled. Gran would need her. And I like working here, she thought, with a sense of discovery. Why *shouldn't* I be assistant manager of a bed-and-breakfast business? I can do my last year of school at the Comprehensive here, and work for Gran in the holidays; Aunt Sarah and Uncle Nick'll just have to agree . . . Funny: I never thought I'd *want* to come back to Wickrithe. She laughed from sheer happiness and saw Ben's face clearing, the pain smoothing out, grey eyes beginning to smile.

"I've ideas for you, then," he said. "There's a lot your Gran could do with her business, if she had a lass like you to help her. She's not that old. A bit o' good weather, and this rheumatism of hers'll clear up. It has before. We'll talk about it when you get back, love."

"All right," said Ruth.

Uncle Nick hit the car horn again, an exasperated blast; and Ben looked guilty. "I'll look after the house, while you're away," he said hurriedly. "I'll get the keys from your Gran, when I go down. And if she needs owt, Ruthie" – he looked away, shyly – "see you tell me. I've money enough. Your aunt and uncle, they've got their family to look after. I can let on to your Gran I've sold that cup for her. No one has to know. I told 'em at the hospital, I knocked me head on the banisters." He looked back at Ruth, eyes pleading like a child's. "I'd best not keep you any more, love – but you *will* come back, won't you – and tell me what it means, this dream of mine?"

"Yes," said Ruth. Looking into his face, she could see what had made Jake his friend. She could tell him everything; like Gran, he would understand.

"Good lass," he said softly. "I'll go now, then, and tell your uncle you'll be down."

"I've only got a couple more locks to check," Ruth said.

He departed, and Ruth turned back to the window. It was at the rear of the house, looking east, and the heavy clouds were continuing to break up.

She'd never thought she would hear of Adam, Jake or Fincara again. I felt I'd lost them for good, she thought; I felt Otherworld was finished for me. And yet it's hardly more than a day since I was there, standing in Murias. However did I manage to forget so soon what it was like – so real, so true?

She had no more doubts now. Otherworld *did* exist, however uncertain one grew, however lonesome and

186

hopeless this world became. Murias is real, Ruth thought, holding the words like a talisman; and one day I'll go back there; Fand said so. She looked from the muddy lane outside into the depth of blue where the clouds had parted. And Gorias would be real, too; one day Adam, Jake and Fincara would come there with the Ildana's Spear, and the eastern sky would break into gold towers; and, thought Ruth, I'll see it, and I'll know they've reached Adam's Paradise.

13513

This book is due for return on or before the last date shown below.

17 SEP 1992